WESTON

The K9 Files, Book 8

Dale Mayer

Books in This Series:

WESTON: THE K9 FILES, BOOK 8
Dale Mayer
Valley Publishing Ltd.

ISBN-13: 978-1-773363-06-6
Print Edition

About This Book

Welcome to the all new K9 Files series reconnecting readers with the unforgettable men from SEALs of Steel in a new series of action packed, page turning romantic suspense that fans have come to expect from USA TODAY Bestselling author Dale Mayer. Pssst… you'll meet other favorite characters from SEALs of Honor and Heroes for Hire too!

Weston was at an impasse in his life, after hearing about his unknown daughter, who'd already been adopted by another family. Only the father had since passed away… So … accepting the mission to track down the missing, blind-in-one-eye, limping K9 dog named Shambhala—in Alaska—was exactly where he needed to be to sort out this other issue in his life. Finding the dog turned out to be easier than Weston had expected, but sorting out how and why this dog's owner's had been murdered was something else again.

Now a widower, Danielle knew her daughter also needed a father, so she'd contacted Weston, not sure if he even knew of the baby's existence. When he said he was on the way, she was concerned at what she'd started and that emotion then turned to terror when Sari's birth mother showed up at Danielle's doorstep, looking for her daughter again.

Things turn ugly when Weston's K9 investigation impacts his daughter's life and her new mother. He must do something, or everything he's finally found will be lost.

Sign up to be notified of all Dale's releases here!
https://smarturl.it/DaleNews

PROLOGUE

WESTON THURLOW WALKED into the offices of Titanium Corp and threw himself down into the big office chair on one side of the boardroom table. "I want in."

Cade looked at Erick, who sat beside him, then across at Weston. "In what?"

"Whatever deal that has all these guys disappearing. I want in on it too."

Erick looked at Cade with a raised eyebrow. They both looked at Weston again. "Say what?"

Weston grinned. "Oh, no. No, no, no. I've been hearing all kinds of stuff," he said, "so no holding back on me."

"All kinds of stuff?" Cade asked. "Can you be more specific?"

"Pierce, Blaze, Zane, Parker, Lucas, even Ethan," he said. "What the heck is going on with them? I heard something about dogs."

"Why are you interested in dogs all of a sudden?" Erick asked, settling back, as if finally understanding.

Just then Badger walked in. "What was that about dogs?" he asked, as he tossed a file in front of Cade. On the top was a picture of Carter, sitting on a railing, a woman's arms wrapped around him and their faces pressed together, both looking deliriously happy.

Cade looked at it and grinned. "And another one bites

the dust."

"Or we could say, *Another very successful story*," Erick corrected, nudging him with his shoulder.

Cade nodded. "Or we could say that. They do look happy together."

"Who?" Weston hopped up to take a look. "Yeah, there's Carter. What the hell has he been up to? And who's the woman?"

"Sister of his best friend," Badger said. "Said he needed to go back and fix a few things, find where his real heart lay."

"Oh, all that mushy stuff," Weston said. "But what kind of jobs are they doing? Do you know how boring it is, day in and day out? All I do is work."

"And yet, here you are looking for another job," Cade remarked with a wry smile. "Ironic, isn't it?"

Weston shrugged. "Yeah, well, it's because I'm bored. Don't you have something else for me to do?"

"Do you have any experience with dogs?"

"Some," he said. "I worked in a K9 unit for a while."

"Only a while?"

"I got promoted," he said. "And then I got blown up. You know how that works. When life takes you down a path you didn't expect to travel." And, of course, he knew they did know. All too well because they'd all been on the same path into the unknown.

Badger smiled at him. "What part of the country are you from?"

"Why?" Weston asked.

"Because we've got dogs all across the country, and we're trying to fit people who have a reason to go someplace to track dogs down in that area." He quickly explained about the K9 program.

Weston's gaze narrowed with interest. "Wow, sounds like a real mess."

"Yep, that's exactly what it is. But we have seven down and five more to go."

"Did they all come to the mainland?" Weston asked.

"You mean in the US?"

He nodded. "Yeah, that's what I'm asking."

"Well, one's in Alaska, one in Hawaii. Does that count?"

He jumped up. "I'll take the one in Alaska. It would be Anchorage, right?"

"Well, that's where it was flown to. But I think it went out to a homesteading family. When a follow-up check was done, they couldn't get a hold of anyone. No one was particularly worried. They tried several times, and honestly nothing might be wrong, but, until someone connects with the owner, the file can't be closed."

"Good, that should be easy enough. Likely they have terrible phone reception out on the homestead, if any at all. The phone is probably off, even if they do have reception. So a simple house call should take care of that," he said. "I'm from Alaska, and I've been looking to visit anyway."

"Did you leave a long-lost love back there too?"

He winced. "Not exactly."

"What does that mean?" Badger asked.

"Well, I left a daughter back there apparently," he said, his voice going superquiet at the old pain rearing its head. "She was adopted out to a very nice family. Only I know that the adoptive mother lost her husband recently. About a year ago." Feeling overwhelmed but in too deep to stop now, he continued, "They, uh, they've been asking me to stop by for a visit because—well, the mother feels my little girl should get to know her dad, now that her other dad is gone."

Weston paused. "She's close to eighteen months old now, and I've never met her."

All the men looked at him in surprise. Dumbfounded, was more like it.

"I know," he said, nodding. "I didn't expect to have a child. But, when a one-night stand ended up telling me a year afterward that she'd had my child and had put it up for adoption, yeah, you could say it wasn't exactly the highlight of my life. I went from fury to grief in a heartbeat and settled somewhere in between."

"Well, we don't pay for these jobs," Badger said, "but there are benefits."

"It doesn't matter," Weston said, his face drawn. "It's time for me to face the music."

"Good," Badger said. "Because the dog up there—her name is Shambhala—and she could really use a calm retirement home."

"Why is that?"

"She's blind in one eye, and she's missing a leg." And, with that, Badger reached for a stack of folders. Flipping through, he pulled out the one in question and handed it to Weston. "You get a copy of that and not a whole lot else."

Weston grinned. "I'll take it."

CHAPTER 1

WESTON KNEW HE'D asked for this. But, as the plane landed in Anchorage, he felt the misgivings ripple through him. It was fine and dandy to be on the side of right and to do the proper thing, but, in this case, he knew it would come with some pain and some sense of not having done the right thing a long time ago. But then it wasn't like anybody had given him the chance to be a father. That opportunity had been taken from him right at the beginning.

If he'd only known about the pregnancy, he could have done things differently, but he hadn't. He hadn't had a choice in the matter, and yet he still felt guilty that his daughter was growing up without him. Not that she was very old, but every day was a day she hadn't had Weston in her life. And that was devastating. Mind-boggling, in a way. It was wrong, but he just didn't know what he was supposed to do about it. Long-term.

He hadn't told the adoptive mother he was coming, and he should have. Daniela Rogers had contacted him a couple times, but he'd held off, not knowing when he'd get there, and then, all of a sudden, it happened, and he was here.

As he stared up at the runway on this early July morning, he realized just how much he both missed and didn't miss this place. He'd spent a lot of years here. Good years.

Weston would have taken his daughter in a heartbeat, if

he'd known about her, and, once again he was back to that—if he'd known—but, at the time she'd been born, he'd been getting blown up. Would knowing have changed any of that? The surgeries? The rehab? No. And no.

It took a good ten minutes for the plane to finally taxi to the gate, and, by the time he made it to the center of the airport, his checked bag had arrived.

With the big backpack he always traveled with tossed over his shoulders, he still hadn't made up his mind as to where he was going first. With a big sigh, he walked out of the airport, heading to the nearest taxi.

A woman stood there, her hands on her hips, studying him.

Okay. Hard to miss her. He raised an eyebrow—noting she was pretty, very pretty; wore a wedding ring, so off limits; but also seemed mad—and was about to walk past when she called out his name.

"Weston?"

He stopped, then turned to look at her and slowly nodded. The adoptive mother. The widow. "Are you Daniela?"

"Why didn't you tell me that you were coming?"

"I figured I'd do that when I got here," he said. "Sometimes traveling doesn't go the way it's expected. How did you know I was coming in?"

"I have my ways," she said.

At that, his second eyebrow went up. "Interesting," he said. "That sounds like you're stalking me."

"No," she said. "I'm not, but, in truth, I'm glad you're here."

"I am too," he said. "I just don't know how it'll work."

"You're here for a job?"

"For you, my daughter and a job. Yes," he said.

6

"But I suppose it was the job that brought you here," she said, her tone turning hard.

His first instinct was to glare at her. His second was to win her over. He sighed. "It's been a rough few months. And the plan was to come, but I was also healing. And I'll be honest. This whole thing has sent me for a loop." At that, her face softened, and he hated that almost more. The last thing he wanted was pity. No place for that in his world. He just felt this need to share with her, to communicate transparently. For Sari. Right?

But he held back going into more details about his unplanned-for exit from navy life. For most people, when they heard about his injuries and his long recovery, sympathy was the first thing that came to mind. That his injuries had been horrific enough a new-to-him but seasoned doctor winced when he brought him up to speed on his last visit didn't help. Multiple compound fractures, soft tissue damage all resulting in several metal plates in his body and now missing a rib. But he'd survived. Still he wasn't completely against Daniela knowing if it softened her attitude toward him because, of course, he should have hopped a plane the minute he had heard about his daughter. But he hadn't. Yet kicking himself more than he already had wouldn't help.

"Well, you're here now," she said, and her smile was a little easier than before.

He studied her for a long moment and then nodded. "That I am. And I apologize," he said. "I had no idea of her existence."

"She's waiting for us at home," she said.

He stopped and looked at her in surprise. "Alone?"

"No, of course not alone," she said, shaking her head. "My sister is there." She motioned toward a double-cab half-ton truck sitting in the lot. "This is mine," she said, already off at a brisk walk, expecting him to follow. She opened the driver's door, then hopped in and waited for him to go around and get in.

He put his backpack on the back seat and hopped in. "I haven't made any plans yet about where to stay."

"I know," she said. "I gather you're one of those 'wing it' kind of guys."

Again, feeling like it was a dig, he bit his tongue. "No," he said mildly. "Like I said, my travel arrangements happened really fast, and I wasn't sure where I would end up, nor what exactly I'd be doing up here."

"Right," she said.

"Will you tell me how you found out I was flying in today?"

"Your landlady," she said briefly.

He stopped, thought about that, then nodded. "Of course Helen would do that."

"Was it top secret?" Daniela asked.

"No, of course not," he said with a half smile. "You just surprised me."

"I used to work for dispatch," she said quietly. "So it was within the realm of possibility that I could track you down."

"Is that how you tracked me originally?" He wondered how he hadn't known she worked for dispatch.

"No," she said. "That was done through the child's mother."

Interesting how everybody avoided using Angel's name. What a dichotomy that moniker was. "I didn't realize you were in contact with Angel," he said.

"I was briefly," she said, "but only at the time of the adoption. I filed the information away and didn't look at it until after Charlie died. Honestly she's not someone I wanted to stay in contact with. It was hard to find her even then to finalize the paperwork. I had to go through multiple people until everything was taken care of."

"You mean, multiple bars?"

She shot him a hard look. "If it was good enough for you to find her there, it was good enough for me to find her there too."

He felt ashamed. "Look. Can we start again?" he said. "I'm Weston Thurlow, and I just arrived in Anchorage. I'm looking forward to meeting Sari and you."

"Sari is looking forward to meeting you too," Daniela said instantly. "And I'm Daniela Rogers. Pleased to meet you finally."

He nodded. "Can we agree it was a bad deal from the beginning?"

"Did you really not know?" she asked curiously.

"I had no idea," he said shortly. "I wasn't very happy when I found out." When she sucked in her breath, he turned toward her. "But not for the reason you think." When Daniela didn't say anything, he forged on. "Look. If I'd known she was pregnant, I would have been there. I don't know if we'd have been together, but I'd have been there. Or, even later, when she decided to bail, I'd have taken responsibility for that baby in a minute, if I'd known."

At that Daniela made a startled exclamation and glanced at him. "Seriously?"

He shot her a hard look. "Absolutely. That's my flesh and blood, and she was given away without me even knowing she existed. How do you think I felt?"

She gave him a second shocked look and then returned to driving, but her face twisted with an expression he didn't know her well enough to understand. "When did you find out?"

"After the adoption was already done," he said quietly. "Angel called me up when she was drunk one night and told me what she'd done. She kept all the details to herself, just letting me know enough to twist the knife."

Again Daniela's breath caught in her throat. "I'm sorry," she said. "That's a hard way to find out you have a child."

"*Had* a child. And it *was* a devastatingly hard way to find out. I've wanted to wring Angel's neck for what she did but couldn't trust myself to be up here."

"You apparently feel strongly about it."

"If you had lost a child, wouldn't you?" He knew his words were wrong when her face blanched. A split-second later he realized that a woman who adopted somebody else's child likely had done so because she couldn't have any of her own.

She gave a clipped nod, and, even though her face was pale, she answered in a controlled tone. "I would have been devastated," she said softly. "I, um, I can't have any children, which is why I adopted Sari."

"Of course," he said. "I really appreciate that you gave her a home."

DANIELA LOOKED OVER at the stranger in her truck. She'd used a lot of persuasion to let his landlady know what their connection was and why she needed to meet him at the airport. So far, he'd rebuffed all her efforts to come meet Sari, but it was for Sari's sake that she was doing this.

At least she thought so. Maybe it was for her own. She

didn't want to examine that too closely. But since her husband's death, Sari hadn't been the same child. It had been hard on the little girl. There was also guilt involved because Daniela had experienced a certain amount of relief knowing Charlie was gone. And how horrible was that?

She stole another sideways glance at the stranger beside her. She shouldn't call him a stranger, since he was the father of her child, and didn't that sound more intimate than it was? She shook her head ever-so-slightly, hoping he wouldn't notice. As she tried to toss off the thoughts confusing her, she glanced at him again. "Are you okay to stay at my place for a night or two, while you get your feet on the ground?"

He shrugged. "It was great that you picked me up. You certainly don't have to give me a place to stay."

"But I have to," she said, "otherwise you might not come over."

He winced at that.

She didn't want to be mean, but, at the same time, she needed to know if there was any connection between her daughter and her daughter's father. It sounded strange to put it that way, but she didn't know how else to say it.

It was another ten minutes before she pulled up to the small, modest two-story house. The main attraction had been a huge backyard, perfect for children to play in. Sari loved having the space. It still broke Daniela's heart that she couldn't give Sari any siblings herself, but she was so grateful to have Sari in her life now that she refused to be upset.

As she parked the truck, she turned to look at him. "My sister's name is Davida," she said, "and she'll probably leave right away."

He looked at her oddly.

She shrugged. "You need to know that a lot of people

here don't have a very good attitude toward you."

He stared at her in surprise.

She nodded and then gave a bit of explanation. "You've got to remember that Angel was here before you. She doesn't have anything nice to say about you."

"Interesting, on Angel's part," he bit off. "I met her one night, and, yes, we had a one-night stand, but two tangoed that night. She never told me about Sari until after the adoption was final." He glared at her. "So, if anybody should be having nothing nice to say, it should be me about Angel."

Daniela didn't answer that but opened the truck door, hopped out and waited for him to join her. He did, his bag in hand, as she walked to the front door.

Sure enough, even before Daniela could open it, Davida had the front door open. She looked at Daniela, then her gaze swung to the six foot, two inch silent male at her sister's side. She took a step back, defensive instincts coming up as she glared at the stranger. "Is this him?" she asked Daniela, her tone hostile.

Daniela sighed. "Yes. This is Weston. But you might want to know a little tidbit here. He didn't know about Sari's existence until after the adoption was final."

Davida turned to look back at the stranger, shock in her gaze. Then, as if not wanting to let go of her anger and resentment, she said, "According to him, you mean?"

"Yes. According to me," he said, standing on the front step. "It'd be interesting to have Angel here, so she could tell a different story with me standing in front of her."

Davida frowned, then glanced back at Daniela. "I haven't seen Angel since you adopted Sari."

"No, thank goodness, neither have I," Daniela said.

Stepping back a little farther, Davida ignored that. "Sari's sleeping."

"Perfect," Daniela said. "I'm glad I'm here for when she wakes up."

With that, Davida grabbed her jacket and purse. "I'll talk to you later." With a hard look at Weston, Davida disappeared out the front door.

CHAPTER 2

D ANIELA TURNED TO look at Weston. "I'm sorry. Like I said, some feelings run deep."

"So do mine," he said in a milder tone. He dropped his bag on the floor, shifted from his coat, placing it on a hook next to the doorway. He looked down at his big boots and sighed. "I guess these need to come off too."

"Yes, please." She slipped off her shoes, parking them to the side. As soon as he had unlaced his boots, placing them next to hers, she asked, "Coffee?"

He stood and gave her a brief smile. "Thank you, that sounds great." He looked around with interest.

She realized he was looking to see what kind of a home she was providing for his daughter. She shrugged self-consciously. "It's not very high-end," she said for lack of other words, "but the reason I rented this house was the big backyard for kids. It's very much a family home."

"Nothing wrong with family homes," he said. "It's obviously the preference, if you've got kids."

She led the way to the kitchen, a huge old country-style room with big counters and wide open with glass doors leading out to the backyard. He walked to the glass doors and stared out.

"City lots. They're not very big." She hated the note of apology in her voice, as if she should have provided Sari with something so much more.

He turned to look at her and smiled. "It's perfect," he said. "I'm sure she is quite comfortable here."

Daniela could feel some of her tension easing until another thought hit her. She didn't know if he had a leg to stand on legally, but she suspected, from hearing his story, he might. And she could feel the fear cloying at the back of her throat at the thought of losing Sari. Daniela kept herself busy, bustling around to put on coffee. "Grab a chair if you want to sit."

He shook his head. "I've been sitting for a while now, so standing is good for a bit."

She could feel that intense gaze on her as she worked. She was hyperaware of everything he did. And the trouble was, he didn't do anything except stare at her. Finally she hit the Start button on the coffeepot, then turned and faced him. "Do you need anything to eat?"

He shook his head.

She frowned. "When Sari wakes up, she'll need a snack."

"That makes sense," he admitted.

She stopped, trying to regain her sense of balance. "Do you have any experience with children?"

His eyebrows shot up. "Are you asking if I left any other abandoned children around the world?"

She glared at him. "No. For all I know, you're married and have kids of your own now."

"Well, I consider Sari my own," he said, calmly crossing his arms over his chest.

She took a deep calming breath. "Look. I feel like we got off on the wrong foot."

"*Again.*" His eyebrows rose ever-so-slightly, but he stared at her steadily.

"I was hoping you and Sari would have a relationship of some kind. She misses Charlie very much."

"What happened to Charlie?"

"Charlie—" she started and then stopped.

He waited, not giving an inch.

She took a deep breath. "Charlie got in his truck one day and drove off a cliff." She could feel the stillness come over Weston.

"Suicide?"

She reached a hand to her chest, trying to still the pain in her heart. "I don't know. It was ruled an accident."

But Weston continued to stare at her steadily. "And what do you think it was?"

"He had a lot of mental health issues," she said. "He was sick, with cancer. He was depressed, on heavy medications, and had mood swings. It's possible either way. He may have done it deliberately. He may have just lost his concentration, or maybe it was just a really bad accident, and no ill intention was behind it."

"And it's easier not to know?"

"Absolutely," she said, "because then I don't have to think about him wanting to leave us. And I don't have to address my feelings about all the years I spent living with someone who was emotionally so difficult."

"So instead," he said with surprising and very piercing insight, "you have to live with the guilt that you could have done more and for feeling relief that it's over."

She stared at him in shock and burst into tears.

HE GAVE A strangled exclamation and abandoned his side of

the island—which was doing a good job of keeping a distance between them—and strode to her. He wrapped her up in his arms, pulling her against his chest. "I'm sorry," he said. "That was uncalled for."

She shook her head and tried to pull away but, at the same time, maintained her grip on his shirt, and so the shirt was coming with her. Finally she gave up the ghost and started to cry deep sobs that soaked his shirt almost immediately.

He held her close, wondering how long it had been since she had had a good cry and if she'd ever had anybody there for her to lean on. Davida sure didn't seem like the warm and fuzzy type. And Daniela had to stay strong for Sari. Weston could already see how Daniela was a protective and nurturing mother figure for Sari.

So it couldn't have been easy to lose her husband, particularly under those circumstances, meanwhile to be looking after Weston's daughter. Not to mention suddenly hearing Sari had been given away without his permission. That was a lot for Daniela to take in all at once.

When she finally stopped crying, she pulled back, wiping her face on her sleeve like a child, the action making him smile. She looked up at him through watery eyes and whispered, "I'm so sorry."

"Don't be," he said, his voice equally quiet. "Sometimes we can bottle it in, but, at some point, it just has to blow."

She sniffled, then turned and washed her hands under the tap. She reached for two cups and, with a slightly shaky hand, poured two cups of coffee.

When she handed him one, he could see she was slowly regaining some sense of control.

"I guess, but, God, this wasn't what you bargained for."

"Still, I'm sorry you've had such a tough year or so."

"Yeah, it has been," she said.

"Well, if you don't mind my asking, why did you want Sari then?"

"Maybe because I was lonely," she said. "Maybe because I was desperate for a child and knew I would never have one of my own. Charlie hadn't fallen ill yet, but I already knew I couldn't have children. Other than that, ... I don't really know, but I saw her and fell in love."

At that, he smiled. "Thank you for that, because you could have given me all the logical answers in the world, but it's the last one that really counts."

She looked at him, and he could see her uncertainty. She'd obviously had a rougher time of it than he knew. She took a deep breath and gave him a real smile, as if somehow they had crossed that barrier that had been upsetting and ruffling feathers when she'd first picked him up. "Sari really is a sweetheart," she said warmly.

"And how did she get along with Charlie?"

"She adored him," Daniela said. "And then, all of a sudden, he wasn't here anymore. And she changed. She became very quiet, introverted in a way she hadn't been before."

"She's hardly old enough to show a lot of that, isn't she?" he asked hesitantly because Daniela was right, he didn't have much exposure to children of that age. To children of any age. He'd been an only child, and no other children were in his immediate world. Another reason why he was completely torn over Sari's current circumstances.

"As a mother, I know," she said. "And it wasn't hard for the people who knew her to see the changes."

"I'm sorry for her then. Grief and loss are hard things to be forced to learn about at that age."

Just then they heard some wailing up above on the second floor. Daniela hopped to her feet and said, "That's Sari."

He got to his feet immediately, and he saw her hesitate.

"If you don't mind, I'd like to get her, calm her down from her nap. Sometimes she wakes up a little edgy. I think it would be best before I introduce the two of you."

He nodded and slowly sat back down again.

As he waited, he looked around, wondering just what the hell he was even doing here. It was obvious she cared and really wanted his daughter, but his concern was, *What did he want?* He already felt like an asshole for not immediately jumping in and starting court proceedings to regain his daughter. Had Sari been adopted legally? That just added to his confusion.

He wanted to be in Sari's life, but, if that were the case, why had he taken so long to get up here? And when he thought about Charlie and what Daniela had been through, this little girl had already lost somebody who cared about her. The worst thing Weston could do would be to step into her life, then step back out again almost as fast. She needed to know he was here for her all the time. This wasn't a case of him being a daddy only when he felt like it. Sari would need him if he would commit. But, if he wouldn't commit, then he needed to get his ass the hell out of this and get a long way away from here.

And it may already be too late for that.

When he heard a sudden noise behind him, he turned to see Daniela holding one of the cutest little cherubs he'd ever seen. She had huge blue eyes, just like his own mother's. And even more damning was the head of bright red hair, but so soft, so thin and fine.

Sari looked at him, and her bottom lip trembled. Then she burst into tears.

CHAPTER 3

D ANIELA CHUCKLED AND held Sari close. "Don't take it personally," she said to the very startled Weston standing, staring in dismay at his daughter. "She doesn't generally take to anybody right off."

He nodded and sank back down again. "It's a good thing I wasn't expecting her to run toward me with open arms," he joked.

She smiled, grabbed his coffee cup, and refilled both hers and his, while she held Sari, cuddling her close.

Finally Sari stopped sobbing, and Daniela sat her daughter on the counter, standing in front of her, Sari with her thumb in her mouth, staring around Daniela at the stranger.

Daniela reached up, gently pulling the thumb from her mouth. "You're just fine now," she said. "This is Weston. Remember? I told you about him."

Sari looked at him with a little more interest and a whole lot less fear as Daniela grabbed Sari once more and moved around the kitchen, making a snack of banana slices for her daughter. She took the plate to the table. With Sari sitting on her lap, Daniela helped her daughter reach toward the plate and pick up pieces to eat. Sari didn't say a word, but now she stared constantly at Weston.

"Now that she's over the initial shock," Daniela said in a quiet voice, "she's contemplating the scenario."

"She doesn't like change, I gather?"

"No, she's had quite a lot of change in her life."

"But she doesn't know I have any impact on her world."

"I think she does," Daniela said. "I understand you're here about a dog?"

At that Sari piped up. "Doggy?" She twisted around, looking in the kitchen for the dog.

Weston chuckled. "I'm here to make sure the dog is doing okay. But I have to track the family down."

"Why is that?"

Weston slowly and quietly, without raising his voice, tried to keep the little girl calm and happy as he explained about Shambhala's life. "She's also blind in one eye," he said, "but, per her file, she's apparently very fond of music."

"That sounds lovely," Daniela said. "But why would she not be with the adoptive family?"

"We just need to contact them to confirm the dog's whereabouts and her well-being because nobody's been able to speak with them. They're homesteaders, so I'll make the trek out to where we believe they are to make sure the dog's doing okay, then come back here and head home again." At that he stopped and frowned.

She nodded. "I know you have to leave," she said. "I was just hoping maybe you would come back and have some kind of a relationship with your daughter."

He looked at Sari, who looked so much like his mom and the pictures he remembered seeing of her when she was a young girl. "She definitely resembles my mother."

"Is your mother still alive?"

He nodded. "Both of my parents are."

"So Sari would have grandparents?" Daniela asked in spite of herself.

"Potentially, yes," he said.

"Potentially?" she challenged.

"Sari's already lost several important people in her life," he said. "Angel and then Charlie. I need to know I can be here in her life on a long-term basis."

She looked at him in surprise. "You know what? I'm really glad you brought that up. I didn't know quite how to tell you, but you need to either be in or you need to ship out."

"I was thinking of that myself," he said. "It's just not all that easy to come to terms with fatherhood when she's already a toddler, and I haven't had that time since her birth or the traditional nine months of pregnancy to get used to the idea."

"I get it," she said. "Still, it needs to be a decision you're prepared to make."

"You obviously feel very strongly about it," he said. "Yet you've gone to a lot of effort to bring me up here."

"That was for Sari's sake," she said.

Just then, Sari looked back at him. "Doggy?"

He looked at her in surprise. "I'm here to look for a doggy, yes," he said cautiously, still not exactly sure how he was supposed to talk to her.

"Doggy," she demanded in a stronger voice.

He smiled, pulled out his phone and brought up the picture of Shambhala. Holding it up for Sari, he said, "Doggy. Shambhala."

Immediately she tried to get her tongue around that twisted word, ending up with *Shamba*.

"Good enough," he said. "I'm here to check on *Shamba*."

Daniela held out her hand. "Do you mind if I see her?"

He shifted his cell over so she could take a look.

She took the phone from his hand and held it at a different angle for better viewing. "You know something? I think I've seen her." She frowned. "Somewhere around the feedstore, I think."

"Maybe the homesteaders were coming in to get something from the store," he said. "They are supposed to be homesteading about ten miles from here."

"What are their names?"

"Grant and Ginger Buckman," he said.

She looked up, her eyes widening. "Oh," she said in a faint voice.

He frowned. "What does that mean?"

"They're dead," she said. "They were killed in a slide about six weeks ago."

He just stared at her.

She nodded slowly. "It was on the news. But I guess the news didn't make it down to where you are."

"Not to mention the fact nobody would know to call us. Any news on the dog?"

"No," she said. "I haven't heard anything about a dog."

"Do you happen to know anybody related to the family?"

She shook her head mutely. "I'm sorry, no."

THAT WASN'T THE news Weston had expected to hear. For some reason he thought this would be a simple drive out to the homestead to see Shambhala was well loved and doing fine. Then he'd drive back, visit with his daughter and escape. But the whole trip was already far more complicated than that.

"I'll contact the police to see if I can get a report on the accident and find out if anybody knows what happened to the dog."

"I have the number for the police," she said, hurriedly standing up. Putting Sari down on the chair, the little girl just sat there and stared at Weston.

He tried a smile, but nothing seemed to work to make her change her expression. Except the photo of the dog. He pulled it up again and said, "*Shamba.*"

The cherub's face split into a happy smile. "Doggy." She tapped the screen. The dog disappeared. She stared up at Weston with her huge eyes, and tears welled up in the corners, her bottom lip trembling.

Immediately he brought the image back up again and showed her. "*Shamba.*"

When his screen went black, he got the same response. And, just as Daniela came running back with a card in her hand, he got the picture up before the waterworks started. She scooped up Sari and smiled as Sari tapped the phone again.

"She appears to like doggies," he said with a wry smile.

"She's also got a mind of her own." Daniela laughed. "She wants what she wants when she wants it."

He wrinkled his nose at that. "I'd say that is probably something all of us would like to achieve—but it's also a family trait," he said. "I'm not necessarily an easy person to get along with either." He looked at the card. "Do you mind if I step out on the porch to make a call?"

She motioned at him. "Please do. I'll get her a little bit more to eat and some milk."

He nodded, smiled and stood. He took the card and

stepped outside and dialed. Behind him, he could hear Sari asking, "Doggy?"

Daniela chuckled. "I guess that's the only thing that's really important to you, isn't it?"

"Want doggy," Sari said, her bottom lip trembling.

"No more tears. Let's get you some milk." She walked over to the fridge.

Weston smiled as he waited on his call to be answered. As soon as somebody did, he identified himself and said he was here at the request of the K9 division, looking into Shambhala's history.

"They owned a dog," the officer said, "but we found no sign of it when we went to the cabin."

"And why did you go there?"

"Standard procedure, to make sure there were no children, visitors, elderly, or pets left behind who would suffer with the loss of this couple."

"And were there?"

"An old cat was in the cabin who didn't take kindly to being removed. It's been adopted through the cat rescue coalition."

"What about the dog?"

"No sign of it. We heard talk of a dog being there but found no sign of her when we were there."

"Do you think it was buried with the truck?"

"The truck wasn't buried. There was a rock slide on the road. They tried to drive around, and the truck went over the edge."

"So, if the dog had been in the back, it could have jumped free?"

"I suppose so," the police officer said slowly, "but I think it would have shown up by now."

"I'm here at Daniela Rogers's place. She thought she saw this dog at the feedstore."

"I hadn't heard anything about that," he said briskly. "Maybe call them and see if they've seen it around."

"I can do that." Weston hesitated and then asked, "Was there anything suspicious about the rockslide accident?"

"No," the cop said, too quickly. "The case was ruled an accident."

Thanking him, Weston hung up and thought about that. Something was definitely off in the officer's tone. But then he didn't know anybody here, and he was an outsider. It could be the detective was just having a crap day and didn't want to be bothered. Or he hadn't done his job and didn't want to have the case be questioned.

Weston brought up the feedstore on his phone, found the number and dialed it. When somebody answered, he explained he was looking for this dog, and it may have been seen around the feedstore.

"A couple dogs have been hanging around but only one recently," he said. "A cream-colored one. She was looking pretty thin though. We put food out at times, if we get a bag that's busted or somehow damaged. We have an awful lot of critters around—skunks, raccoons and the like—so who knows how much these skittish dogs may ever get of it."

"Okay," he said. "Are you against me coming in with a big crate and trying to catch her to see if it's the one I'm looking for? If she's not, I'd still like to get her to a rescue to help her."

"It'd be nice if you could rescue her," he said, "but we can't get close enough to really help any of them."

"Well, surely rescue groups would come in and help, right?" Weston asked.

"We called them early on. They tried a couple times but didn't get anywhere."

"Do you know what breed the cream-colored dog is? Does she have only three legs?"

"From what I can remember, she's kind of shepherd looking but not quite. And yes on only having three legs. That's partially why everyone here was giving her handouts. They felt sorry for her."

"Yes, that's likely her then," Weston said. "I'm coming into town. I should be there within the next two hours."

"We'll see you then."

CHAPTER 4

AFTER HEARING WESTON'S plan, Daniela hesitated and then asked, "Do you want me to go with you?"

Weston looked at her, surprised, then glanced down at Sari, who was snuggled up against her mom again. "You don't have to," he said gently. "I know you need to be with her."

"That's the thing about little ones," Daniela said with a smile. "She comes with me too."

He laughed at that. "Not to mention the fact I don't have wheels at the moment either," he said with a nod. "So, if you don't mind, I'll accept your generous offer."

"Good enough," she said. "We can leave in thirty if you'd like. Puts us there a little early but not too much"

"Is that a problem? I can work with your timeframe. It really doesn't matter when we get there. I had to give them a timeframe and I hadn't asked you."

She shook her head. "No, not at all. It's fine." She seemed to come to a decision as she stood and said, "Would you mind straightening up the kitchen, while I take Sari to the bathroom and grab her a sweater?"

"No problem," he said. He started clearing away the dishes.

She noted how he turned to watch the two of them walk from the room. She had to hand it to him. This was a pretty strange event in his life, but he appeared to be handling it. She was a little disoriented by the conversation about needing to be all in or all out because she'd had the same thought herself. It never really occurred to her that he might choose to be all out. Mostly because she didn't want him to.

At the same time though, he was correct. Sari had already lost Charlie and Angel. Sari was young and would adapt, but Daniela hoped Weston would want to stay in his daughter's life. He didn't look like somebody who'd spent his life around nieces and nephews, and that made the adjustment that much harder for him. Not that she was making any excuses because, if there was ever a time for somebody to step up, it was when he found out he was a father. And yet complications for him arose, since he hadn't found out until he'd already lost all access to the child. That was the part that really bothered her.

She had wanted him to meet Sari because she thought it was the right thing to do for her little girl. But now, maybe she was trying to give him a role in his daughter's life because he'd had it taken away. It certainly wasn't the story Angel had told her. But then, Angel was that kind of a person.

He was right. Angel was a bar-hopping party girl who lied to make ends meet and to make the world revolve around her in the way she wanted it to. Not the easiest of people to get along with.

Daniela placed Sari on the toilet-training seat. The little girl was doing really well. Daniela had wanted to potty train Sari early, and sometimes she managed, and sometimes she didn't. Daniela had been happy to wait until Sari was a little bit older, but Sari had a mind of her own. When she was done, Daniela helped her off the seat, cleaned her up and pulled up her clothes. Washing her hands, she ran a comb over both of their heads and then picked Sari up and carried her downstairs, where she put on her coat.

Weston stood at the door, waiting for them, his bag in hand.

"Are you bringing your bag too?" she asked with a frown.

He raised his eyebrows. "I can hardly just stay here at your generosity," he said. "I need to get some wheels at least, and I need to find a place to stay."

"Oh," she said, staring down at Sari.

"I don't want to be a burden," he said gently.

She looked up, flashed him a bright smile and said, "You won't be."

He hesitated, and she realized he really wasn't sure about staying with her.

"It's okay, you know?" she said. "It would be a good chance for you and Sari to be together."

He nodded and then dropped his bag, tucking it by the wall. "In that case, thank you. But I still need to get some wheels."

Feeling much better, she nodded. "That makes sense, if you've got a bunch of running around to do. I'm sure it would be nice to be independent."

"Always," he said.

She went to open the front door, but he stepped ahead of her, opened it and let them go through. As she walked down the front steps, he called out, "You lock the door, right?"

She looked back at him with a shrug. "I never do."

When he frowned at her, she chuckled. "It's Alaska, not Detroit."

"I hear you," he said, as he walked toward the sidewalk

with a smile.

"I LOCKED IT anyway," he said.

She shrugged. "Good thing I have a key hidden and keys on me. Otherwise I wouldn't have thanked you for that."

"Maybe not, but I'd still feel better to have it locked." He hopped into the passenger side of the front seat and watched as she buckled his daughter into the back. It was still something for him to get used to. His little girl looked up at him and said, "Doggy."

He chuckled. "You have a one-track mind."

"Doggy."

"We'll go see what happened to the doggy," he said.

Daniela hopped into the front seat, turned on the engine and pulled out of the driveway. "Where do you want to go first?"

"I'd rather check out the feedstore first," he said. "I guess it's a slim chance the dog is still there, but, if that was the last sighted location, then that's our best bet."

"And then what?" she asked as she turned the truck onto the main road.

"I need to get a set of rental wheels, so, if you can drop me off there, I'll pick up a truck and probably take a drive out to Grant and Ginger's place."

"We might as well do that after the feedstore," she said. "No point in us taking two vehicles out there."

"Or you could go home," he said gently, "and spend some quality time with Sari."

She snorted at that. "We're trying to spend quality time with you, if you hadn't noticed."

He had the grace to feel bad about that. "I just don't know how long I'll be, and it might be boring." He glanced back at Sari, who was staring at him with a passionate look in her eye. "Yes, doggy, I know," he said before she could. The little girl beamed at him. He laughed. "She is quite the manipulator already."

"She is, indeed," Daniela said. "I think all kids are."

"Never been around them," he said.

"This is your chance," she said.

"I can hardly relocate to Alaska," he said. "It's not like finding dogs is my typical kind of work."

"What is your kind of work?"

"*Hmm.* Guess I need to think about that. It's a little hard to describe, and you're right. I was healing and trying to forge a new path for myself. I've been helping out a group, finding work for veterans. Then I heard about a bunch of people doing searches for these dogs. When I found out one was up here, I asked for the assignment."

She smiled at that revelation and filed it away to think about later. "Still, it seems strange to me that the government would shut down such an important program."

He looked at her with a wry smile. "Does it really surprise you?"

"Maybe not," she admitted. "It always seems like the money's going in the wrong direction when the government is involved."

"Lots of times it does," he said. "So, in this case, we're trying to make sure the dogs end up having a good life."

"Doggy," came the voice of the very single-track-minded little girl in the back seat.

Both adults laughed. It was only a fifteen-minute drive to the feedstore, and Weston looked around with interest.

"It's been a few years since I was here," he said. "I have to admit. It doesn't look like it's changed much."

"It grew a little," she said, "then the stock market contracted, and some of the stores shut down. I think the population has stayed the same over the last ten years, and the businesses changed some, depending on what could make a go of it."

"Exactly. I'm sure the cruise ports are still making big money, aren't they?"

"More than big money when it comes to the overall economy," she said quietly. "But there's almost a love-hate relationship with them."

"I think that's the same the world over," he said.

Before long she took a series of turns and pulled into a large parking lot. At the end of the parking lot was a feedstore.

He looked at it and said, "I don't think I've ever been in this one."

"It hasn't been in this location long," she said. "It was in town before but much smaller."

"Maybe that's why," he said as he hopped out. He stopped and looked around and saw some trees lining the parking lot and a wooded area off another hundred yards or so. "I suppose the dog could be hiding in there," he said, as he pointed toward the woods.

She looked at him as she leaned into the back and unbuckled Sari from the car seat. "Sure," she said. "But I'm sure they are also hunting the alleyway, looking for anything edible."

"That's very possible," he admitted. "This dog's not exactly used to hunting and hasn't ever been allowed to hunt for her own food."

"I guess the dog's been fairly regimented with its K9 training, right?"

"The K9 training can vary, depending on what the dog will do. In this case, she was use to sniffing out IEDs and people. Though I'm sure a certain amount of survival training was included in that."

She nodded, and, with Sari in her arms, they walked toward the front of the building. He kept searching out the side area, looking for any sign of a dog.

Inside, the place bustled with business. He waited until he could get one of the guys' attention.

"Can I help you find something, sir?"

"I called about thirty minutes ago but ended up coming straight here," Weston said, "about a dog I'm looking for."

A look of recognition appeared on the guy's face. "Oh, right, that was me you were talking to. Come on. I'll show you where we usually see them." He led the way to the back. "The dogs are usually seen in this area, but I haven't seen any today."

"That's always the way, isn't it?" Weston said.

The younger man laughed. "Exactly. But go ahead and call her, and see if you can get any to come in closer."

"Do you have dog treats inside?"

"All kinds," the kid said. He pulled out an open package from behind a register at the back door. "We often give them the treats from here. So go ahead and grab a bunch, if you think it'll help you get close to the dog."

Weston reached out his hand and grabbed several. Leaving Daniela and Sari inside the building, he walked toward the rear parking lot. He started calling for the dog, using the same military whistles she would be used to. An almost weird stillness filled the air, but no dog came running as he walked past the vehicles parked in front of pallets of feed still to be taken into the warehouse.

Then he thought he caught a furtive movement. Pausing to let his eyes adapt to the strange scenery around him, he caught the same movement off to the right. Slightly he turned to watch and could see a dog in between the pallets, staring at him. He crouched down slowly. "Shambhala?" And then ordered her, "Come."

The dog bared her teeth and backed away, and he saw her missing back leg. If he needed a sign this was the dog, that was it.

"Shambhala," he said, his voice firm but neutral.

The dog hesitated, growling, obviously confused and not certain about what to do. Weston took two steps forward, and her hackles rose, and she resumed growling.

Then he noted the dried blood on her shoulder. He frowned, then crouched down again. "Shambhala, come here."

The dog whined and took a hesitant step toward him.

He nodded and held out his hand with a dog treat. "Come." Obviously the training was warring with the dog's instinct for survival and her need to run away from any threat. He could only surmise how much of the last few weeks of her life had been a fight and how difficult it would have been for her. Still it was obvious she still responded to her training. He kept his voice firm and calm as he talked to her.

"You've had a pretty rough time of it, haven't you?" he asked, his voice neutral.

When she took another step toward him, he smiled and held the treat out farther.

She stretched her neck out, sniffing.

Then he put it on the ground in front of him, took one step back and crouched down again. "Shambhala, come."

She took several more hesitant steps closer to the dog biscuit and him, still fighting off her training, and yet, at the same time, understanding somewhere in the back of her mind this was what she used to do.

He waited until she got closer, then he said, "Stop." Immediately the dog froze, quivering. He smiled at her gently, then said, "Okay."

She bent lower to the ground, snatched the treat and inhaled it.

He hated to see she was obviously starving. He pulled out a second dog treat out, knowing she needed much better food than just this, but it was something. Giving her almost no time, he held it out, put it down a little bit closer, took a half a step back and waited until she came.

As soon as she got there, he ordered her to stop.

She quivered and glared at him, hating the command, but helpless to override her training. Then he released her to have the treat. She gobbled it up and seemed to relax slightly.

He had a third one in his hand. This time he didn't pull back but placed it between them. As soon as she got there, she hesitated, waiting for him to give her the command. He smiled and told her it was okay.

She gobbled it up and then looked at him again. He had a couple little pieces in his hand still, but that was it. He held out his hand with the pieces on his flat palm, his fingers outstretched, the treat on the surface.

Sensing some trick, she froze, wanting the last little bit, but not sure she could trust him. He kept talking to her in a calm gentle voice. He had looped a rope over his arm so as soon as he could get closer to her, he would drop it around her neck. She stepped up a little closer and closer again.

He kept talking to her calmly and gently. In the background he could hear little Sari's voice calling out for the doggy. But neither he nor Shambhala broke eye contact. It was too important right now.

She took another step forward and sniffed his hand, wanting the treat, but it was just a hair out of reach. He kept still and kept talking to her. As soon as she reached for the treat, he eased his spare hand up under the rope and carefully looped it over her neck. She froze as soon as the noose dropped down, then looked at him in shock.

He stood up slowly and gently, told her to heel. With the leash on, she stepped up to his left side and stood at attention. He reached a hand down and gently stroked the top of her head.

"That's a good girl, Shambhala," he whispered. He walked her back toward where Sari and Daniela waited for him. Sari had a biscuit in her hand and so did Daniela. He held out his hand for the one from Daniela. She gave it to him. He turned to face Shambhala and ordered her to sit. She did. He held up part of the treat for her.

"She looks starved," Daniela murmured at his side. Then took Sari's treat from her to hand to Weston.

He fed Shambhala the remaining treat. "Looks like she's had a pretty rough time," he said. "Maybe just since the accident, I don't know. But there's blood on her haunch too."

"You seem to have her under control now," she said in surprise. "You made that look easy."

"Nothing easy about it," he said. "That's her training. She's responding to the command style she knows."

"Maybe, but she still looks like she has suffered."

With that all the treats were gone. Shambhala looked up at him as if to see what was next. He smiled at her and reached a hand down to scratch her ears. "We need to find a place where we can take you, girl."

"I have a fenced yard," Daniela said.

He looked at her and hesitated. He'd already taken advantage of her generosity, more than he would have liked. It was as if she could sense his hesitation.

"Look. No reason not to," she pointed out quietly. "I know you're trying to be independent, but you need a place where the dog can be safe. I do have a good fence, and she needs a few days to recover. What will you do with her after this?"

"I don't know," he said in surprise. "I didn't allow myself to think to this point. Honestly, I wasn't sure I'd catch her."

"And here I thought you always had everything planned out," she said in a light teasing manner.

He didn't take his gaze off Shambhala, who was much more relaxed now. He gave her a hand command to lie down, and she dropped and lay down. When he gave her another one to relax, to say she was off duty, she sprawled out on her side. "She is very well trained," he said.

"I don't know if you just made her do that last bit," Daniela said, "but, if you did, that's amazing. I'm surprised she remembers any of that training."

"It's not a case of remembering as much as it was what she was. It was how she lived for the longest time, so anything other than her training would have been uncomfortable and scary. This is giving her that sense of security and routine again."

"Well, it's obvious you've won her over."

He nodded. "Yes, but she needs real food." He hesitated and looked back at the feedstore and could see the same young man, watching him in astonishment. "I'll need a large bag of dog food," he said. "Something extremely high in protein, if you have it. I can give you a credit card, "he said. "I don't want to leave her or take her inside just now."

The young man nodded. "No problem. I'll carry it out. Where to?"

Daniela stepped back, smiling at him. "In my vehicle over here."

"Doggy!" Sari screamed, clearly on the verge of being upset.

Daniela hesitated, looking at Weston.

He held out his hands. "If you want to be close to the doggy," he said, "you have to be quiet, and you have to sit nicely."

Sari looked up at him and reached out her arms. And, just like that, for the first time ever, he picked up his daughter and held her in his arms. It didn't matter that her entire focus was on the dog at his feet because his entire focus was on her. And that special smell, a sense of holding a small and precious life, that sweet innocence, it was so hard to even understand what he felt, but Sari had just such a sense of wonder and lightness about her.

She bounced on his hip and laughed at the doggy. Shambhala looked up at her, not disinterested but more curious, as if she hadn't had any exposure to children either.

"You and me both," Weston said to the dog. He held his daughter firmly but with a little hesitancy. She appeared to have absolutely no fear of falling and completely trusted he would hold her. The trouble was, she was small, slippery and moved very quickly. He knew he'd get the hang of it, but, at the moment, it was like holding a wiggling eel as she kept leaning down toward the dog. He crouched with her in his arms and told Shambhala to guard. Immediately she stood up and sat down, attentive now. But she looked at him curiously, as if to say, *Guard what?*

It wasn't the best command Weston could have given Shambhala, but he'd been looking for something to make her pay attention as he held his daughter a whole lot closer.

"Sari, this is Shambhala."

"*Schambach*," his daughter mumbled happily. She clapped her pudgy hands together and waved them in Shambhala's face.

Shambhala looked at Sari, as if she were an oddity. But Shambhala was completely relaxed and calm around Sari. For that he was grateful.

When he could, he reached out a hand to gently stroke Shambhala's head and scratch behind her ears. Then he held out one of Sari's hands for the dog to smell. Shambhala gave them both a good sniff and then lay back down again. He put Sari on her feet, not sure how well she walked, and she leaned forward, reaching for the dog's ear. He showed her how to gently pet the top of the dog's head and to stroke Shambhala's ears. Sari was beyond delighted and chortled happily every time she touched the dog. She wasn't sure what was going on, but it was obviously something she was desperately enjoying.

But that didn't mean he knew the dog enough to trust Shambhala with his little girl's life. He had assumed Shambhala would guard and look after her, but what if the child accidentally hurt the dog? Would Shambhala accept it as a young person's accident, or would the dog turn on Sari? Again, the dog was an unknown. She might have been well-trained, but she'd also suffered. It was hard to say what the outcome would be.

Behind him, he could hear Daniela's voice. "Weston, the dog food is loaded."

"Okay," he said, standing up with Sari in his arms. Sari screeched and tried to get back down to the dog. "She's really hung up on Shambhala," he said.

"But is it safe for her?"

"I don't know," he answered honestly. "This is the first I've met the dog too."

"That's the problem," Daniela said. "I get that she's well-trained. I just don't know what she's like around a child."

"I know," he said, "it's an unknown situation." As he stepped away, Sari cried out some more. "She's really focused on the dog," he said with some concern.

Daniela stepped up to his side, reached out to take Sari from his arms and walked firmly back into the store with the little girl screaming. He looked down at Shambhala, reaching for the rope again. "Come, Shambhala."

The dog hopped up and walked at his side. Weston walked around the building to where the truck was parked. There he had to make a decision about bringing her inside or putting her in the back of the bed. There was no canopy to keep her in safely, and loose inside the bed of the truck was not something he was willing to risk. But the car seat was in the back seat. Still, that was probably where the dog was better off. He looked at Daniela. "Do you want to move the car seat to the front?"

Daniela frowned and said, "Maybe if you want to put the dog in the back, you should sit back there too."

He nodded. "That's a good way to handle this." He

opened the door to the back seat, sat beside his daughter and then Shambhala jumped up on the other side of him.

Daniela hopped into the front and said, "Your credit card and receipt are here, by the way."

"Thanks, I'll grab it when we get out," he said.

She didn't say anything but started up the engine. "Now that you have the dog," she said, "what do you want to do next?"

"I want to get a set of wheels."

"Will you be staying on?"

He looked at her. "Why wouldn't I?"

CHAPTER 5

D ANIELA DIDN'T KNOW what to say. "I thought you were only coming to get the dog, and you've already accomplished that."

"No, not necessarily," he said. "We found the dog, yes, but I don't really know what the circumstances are, and what's best for her. So that'll take a bit to figure out."

She smiled and relaxed slightly. "I hear you," she said. "I guess I was hoping you wouldn't turn around and take off right away."

"No, that's not the plan," he said.

Her smile brightened, then she nodded and drove out of the parking lot. "Good. A rental agency is up here, if that's okay?"

"As long as it's one of the big companies, it will be fine," he said.

Once she had parked, he hopped out and went inside. Daniela got Sari out of her car seat and held her as a precaution, not knowing how Shambhala would react with Weston gone.

Once inside, Weston asked to rent a truck, preferably one with a large cab and a canopy. It took about fifteen minutes to get the paperwork done, and he came out with a set of keys. Walking to the back seat, he pulled out Shambhala, then turned and walked around to where

Daniela was buckling Sari back in.

"I'll take the dog to the police station to make sure there's no paperwork involved in keeping her, and then I'll head back to your place."

"What about going out to Grant and Ginger's house?"

He frowned. "I forgot about that. I guess I'll wait and see what the cops say, then maybe head there next. It wouldn't be a bad idea to see if Shambhala has things there. Maybe she needs to find some closure herself."

"That's probably a good idea. On the other hand, I don't know about just leaving the two of you alone."

"Why not?" he asked with a frown.

She shrugged. "I get the feeling you can get into trouble without much effort."

He chuckled. "Maybe so, but we'll be okay."

She looked at Sari and said, "Maybe I'll just take her home then."

"Is there anything you need for the next couple of days that I can pick up?" he asked.

She shook her head. "I'll just pick up a few groceries on my way home."

"Well, here. Let me give you some money at least," he said, pulling out his wallet, and he gave her a few hundred dollars. "Go ahead and stock up on whatever you need. I'm pretty low maintenance. I can live on coffee, bread and something for sandwiches. A steak once in a while."

She nodded and smiled. "I can handle that."

"Okay, give me an hour or two." He checked his watch. "I'll give you a call and check in." With that, he said goodbye and headed to his new vehicle.

WESTON LOADED SHAMBHALA into the front seat of the rental truck and hopped into the driver's seat. He could see that Daniela was heading back out the way they had come, while he was heading to the police station.

As soon as he got there, he parked and took Shambhala out, still with just the rope on her, and walked up to the front door. Once inside, he asked to speak to Detective Kruger. The woman looked at him in surprise. "I spoke to him about this dog earlier."

She nodded and told him to wait a moment. She made a couple calls, but Weston couldn't hear what was going on. A few minutes later he looked up to see a salt-and-pepper-haired man walking through a side door with his hand out.

"I'm Detective Kruger," he said.

Weston smiled, shook his hand and introduced them. "This is Shambhala."

He looked at the dog in surprise. "Wow. How did you get a hold of her so fast? You appear to be on first-name basis already." He studied the dog. Shambhala was alert but not aggressive.

"We found her behind the feedstore," Weston said. "I was hoping to take a trip up to Grant and Ginger's place, take a look around to see just how Shambhala was living."

The detective nodded. "That's fine with me, and no-body's living there at the moment."

"Did they own the property?"

"Yes, it appears they did," the detective answered. "We contacted Grant's brother, Gregory, but haven't heard anything since."

"Right," Weston said. "If you're not from Alaska, it would be hard to know what to do with property up here, I suppose."

"Exactly."

Weston handed over a Titanium Corp business card with his cell phone number and his name written on the back. "If you get any information on the case, I'd appreciate knowing about it."

"You don't think their deaths have anything to do with the dog, do you?"

"Not sure, I just want to make sure it doesn't," Weston said.

"And if it does?" the detective challenged.

Weston frowned at him. "I'm staying at Daniela Rogers's place. She's adopted my daughter. The last thing I want to do is introduce any danger to them."

"Is picking up a dog that's been running wild going to do that?" the detective asked with a frown.

"I want to make sure that's not the case." On that note, he said, "We'll head out now, so we can get back in time for dinner." As he turned away, pulling Shambhala's rope, he noticed she seemed to be keeping an eye on a nearby detective a little too closely. Was it his suit? Bringing back memories of her old life?

Weston and the dog walked back outside, where they both hopped into the front seat of the rental truck. Weston pulled up his GPS and plugged in the address where Shambhala had been staying. It was a good twenty minutes there as he had to cross town, but then they'd been homesteading, so that made sense. He set the GPS for directions, and, following the computerized voice, he headed out toward Shambhala's old home. Almost as soon as they hit the outskirts of town heading in the right direction, Shambhala sat up with interest.

"I'm sorry you can't stay out there anymore, girl," Weston said. "It just won't work now."

Shambhala didn't appear to notice what he was saying, and the closer they got to the homestead, the more she seemed to relax and to be more comfortable inside the vehicle. When he turned onto the driveway, she barked excitedly.

"They're not here now," he murmured. If the dog didn't know her owners were gone, this wouldn't be the homecoming she wanted.

Sure enough, when they got to the place, he opened the truck door, and she jumped out and raced up to the front porch. She started to whine, then jumped up on the door, which creaked open. It was a single-story log-cabin-style home with a couple bedrooms off the back. He walked in to see just the barest of furnishings and no obvious signs of anybody having lived here in several weeks.

Shambhala raced through the cabin, whining and barking, obviously searching for her family.

Weston leaned against the door, hating to see her anxiety and her sense of loss, but it was better if she got used to this now.

She came back, looking for them still, then darted out the front door and headed to the fields. Weston followed, giving her a chance to check out everything she could because that was the only way for her to come to terms with it.

Finally, after twenty minutes of checking all her favorite spots and the places she expected to find her family, Shambhala came back with her tail down. The look in her good eye when she stared at Weston almost broke his heart. He hopped down so he was sitting on the small deck and reached out a hand to gently scratch the back of her head and to hold her.

"They would have come back if they could have," he murmured, "but they couldn't."

Shambhala didn't seem to understand what he said, but then why would she? He didn't even understand the truth of all this. He only knew what the detective had told him. And, in his heart of hearts, he hoped it was as simple as that, but he wasn't so sure it would be.

With Shambhala at his side, they did a search of the house, garage and another outbuilding, then walked through the fields. In the six weeks the family hadn't been here, nature was already taking over. Weeds were everywhere, and, if vegetables had been planted here, they were quickly being incorporated back into the landscape.

Weston found no tractor equipment, no vehicles, just whatever had been here at the time they died. And, for that reason alone, he figured Shambhala must have been in the vehicle at the same time when the Buckmans died. He collected the dog dishes, the couple toys he saw and a collar and leash hanging off the door. He put them on her then headed toward the rental truck, whistling for her. She was still racing around but finally stopped, looked around one last time and ran to him. He opened the driver's side door; she hopped in and moved over to the passenger side.

"At least we got that done. I'm sorry it wasn't better news."

He drove out farther, looking for the location where the slide occurred, wanting to see where the accident had been.

As they got close, the dog started to growl. Finding that reaction odd, Weston pulled off to the side of the road, and, slipping the leash on her neck to keep track of her, he hopped out.

It was a little farther down, maybe another fifty yards, but he stopped because it was obvious parts of a rockslide and a vehicle had been crushed underneath the rocks. Part of it had been removed but part of it was still wedged under some rocks. The dog started to whine.

"I know, Shambhala, but it's too late for them." He knew no bodies were left in the vehicle, and they were back in the morgue or had already been buried by now. He studied the marks on the road, wondering if it really had been an accident. He hated to think it was anything other than that, but it was just way too possible. And, with a final look, he called Shambhala. "Come on, girl. Let's go home."

CHAPTER 6

D ANIELA HEADED TO the grocery store. She admitted she'd stayed a little too long, watching Weston in the rental place, trying to figure out what it was about him that moved her so. Was it the connection she could see to her daughter? Because that could be a dangerous path. She'd been the one to push for a relationship, as little Sari had already suffered enough loss in her life.

But just something about the man himself made her breath catch in the back of her throat. Almost like a cord from her led to him, and she desperately wanted to stay attached, and that was even scarier. She and her husband had had a decent life, until he'd changed. She wasn't sure if she should blame that change on his illness or the girlfriends she'd found out about, but it had changed her perspective. Having little Sari as part of her life had been a gift that she'd wanted forever, and she had been willing to put up with a lot in order to have it.

But, when she lost Charlie, she realized just how much compromise she'd made in order to have the perfect little family she thought she'd always wanted and needed. Her definition of family was changing now. It was just her and Sari, and yet Daniela knew Sari could definitely benefit from having her father in her life. Particularly now that Daniela realized he wasn't a man who had intentionally walked away from his daughter.

She understood Weston's need to have time to adjust, now that he knew about Sari. She imagined a man like that didn't take betrayal easily. Hell, nobody did, nor should they. Betrayal was at the core of every failed relationship. People made choices on a day-to-day basis on whether they would be a good person or a shitty person.

When Charlie had gotten ill, he'd gone on this wild rampage of trying everything he thought he'd missed out on in his life, including affairs. She hadn't understood, and he'd thought she should have. Charlie had made an agreement that he would be decent while the child was around, but, other than that, he wanted to be free to go his own way.

At that point, Charlie wasn't the most levelheaded, easygoing, honorable man. She thought he had been when they first married, but maybe the marriage itself had changed him somehow. It was also pretty disconcerting to realize she no longer cared. He had ruined everything between them, not only ruined it all but killed it dead.

It was hard for her to find any regrets in the way their relationship ended. She could grieve for the man he had been, but that man had died a long time ago. She felt like a terrible person for even thinking along those lines, but, how else was she to take this, when somebody became the worst of the worst in front of you and then treated you like dirt right up to the end with no explanation? Well, except that maybe some blame had been involved. She didn't understand that, but maybe Charlie blamed Daniela because she was alive and healthy, and he wasn't. He never did voice that complaint or his anger and frustration as to why, but it had left her with a very bitter taste.

His affairs and complete lack of regard for her well-being

had made life difficult. But she'd stuck by his side right to the bitter end. Maybe she shouldn't have; maybe she should have taken Sari and run, but that wasn't her way. Unfortunately it seemed to be the way of the world, but she didn't have to sign up for being that way herself.

As she walked into the grocery store, she picked up a few things for Sari, wondering if Weston was serious about pulling up stakes. She added a few other items she needed for the house. As she pulled up to the checkout line, a woman behind her started talking.

"Daniela, I'm surprised to see you here."

She felt something inside close down. It was Trudy. Another one of her husband's wild flings near the end of his life. Turning, with a bright plastic smile, she said, "I don't know why you'd be surprised. It's the closest grocery store to my house."

Trudy just shrugged, completely oblivious to the animosity Daniela was trying hard to keep tamped down. "How are you doing?" Trudy asked.

If Daniela didn't already know about the affair, she might actually think Trudy cared, but Daniela did know because her husband was always extremely explicit about his antics. "I'm fine," she said. "Why wouldn't I be?"

"Well, after Charlie—" and she dropped her voice into a hostile whisper.

Several other people were around them, and Daniela could see their interested glances. She didn't recognize anybody, but she could feel her temper spike. Why would this woman do this? How two-faced could one person be?

She smiled again at Trudy. "I guess I should thank you for giving him his little fling at the end of his life then, huh?"

Trudy's eyes widened. Flustered, she said, "Sorry? I don't

know what you mean."

"What do you mean, *you don't know?* Come on, Trudy. Charlie was pretty desperate to try out a few other women before he died," she said smoothly. "I understand you were one of them, so I guess I should say thank-you for helping him get through his last few days."

Trudy's face flushed bright red and then paled. She looked horrified. "I don't know why you would think that."

"Because he told me, of course," Daniela said in a reasonable tone. "We went over the long list of what he considered his conquests. Didn't he tell you what he was doing? That he was having his last little hurrah?"

Trudy swallowed hard, desperately trying to get out of the checkout line, now as even more people crowded around.

"I don't know what you mean," she said faintly.

"Well, shake your memory," Daniela said. "Just like you shook your bootie for him."

And, with a heavy gasp, Trudy turned and swung her cart away, racing down the aisle.

Wearing a smirk, even as she was admonishing herself for being such a bitch, Daniela turned to face the checker. But the woman had a commiserating look on her face, as did several other people in her line.

"That couldn't have been easy," the woman murmured, as she rang up the items. "But honestly, that woman is a menace."

"Oh, her reputation precedes me, does it?"

One of the women farther down the line of shoppers said, "Absolutely. It's part of who she is."

"So maybe I really should thank her," Daniela said with a laugh. "At least my husband died with a smile on his face."

At that, the other people weren't sure if they should

laugh with her or be horrified at her comment. She gave a slight wave of her hand. "Don't mind me," she said. "I'm still adjusting to, well, to a lot of things."

At that, they instinctively turned sympathetic and nodded. She paid for her purchases, and, with Sari sitting quite happily in the cart seat, walked back to her truck.

Daniela didn't even know why she'd done it. She wasn't someone who wanted the world to know about her dirty laundry. But something had been just so fake and so downright mean about Trudy's original comment that Daniela couldn't stop herself. It made no sense. Because she normally wasn't that kind of a person, although maybe she needed to be. Maybe something about her husband's about-face personality change made her stop and look at herself. She hated the idea she still had a lot of hurt she held inside. Hurt she needed to let go of, or it would ultimately hurt Sari too.

As soon as Daniela had Sari packed up in the truck, and she started the engine, she took several deep breaths to calm down. Then realized her hands were shaking. Tears came to her eyes, and she sat here for a long moment, listening to Sari babble in the back seat.

She was full of sadness, soberly contemplating life choices and how difficult some of them were. Nobody had known how bad her marriage to Charlie was at the end. Nobody but her and Charlie. Even her sister hadn't known. When her phone rang, she picked it up off her purse to see it was her sister.

"What the hell just happened?" her sister asked.

Daniela groaned. "What are you talking about?"

"The conversation you just had in that grocery store."

"Well, that didn't take long. Who told you?"

"A school friend," she said. "She saw you there and heard the conversation."

"Of course she did," Daniela snapped. "And, of course, gossip travels faster than the speed of sound, doesn't it?"

"Not quite." Davida's tone was grim. "Why didn't you tell me?"

Daniela gave a bitter laugh. "Because I was going through enough shit at the time without listening to more."

That stopped her sister cold. "I wouldn't have given you shit about it," she said slowly.

"Yes, you would have. You would have made sure I left him or argued every day about me leaving him."

"It was bad enough what you went through," her sister said, "but to think he had an affair with Trudy?"

"Trudy was one of eight," Daniela said, her tone grim, as she decided there was no point in keeping secrets anymore. "When Charlie got ill, he switched personalities. I don't know if it was the medications, his mental illness or what, but he became a completely different person. He was verbally abusive, and then he started having affairs. It was as if he was desperately eager to sample everything he hadn't sampled so far and was running out of time."

"And the sampling was with other women?" Davida asked incredulously.

"Yes," Daniela replied, "among other things."

"Like?" her sister asked cautiously.

"Getting drunk to the point of puking, waking up with a heavy hangover every day. Doing a lot of drugs, and not knowing where he was from one moment to the next," Daniela said quietly. "He even tried staying up for three days in a row because he didn't want to miss a single moment."

"Jesus," her sister said.

"No way I could tell you," Daniela said. "The questions would have been endless, and there was nothing I could do but push it all down. Once Sari came into my life, I wouldn't do anything to jeopardize her life. You know that."

"And I suppose that perfect husband of yours made some deal with you, about you staying by his side, didn't he?"

"Maybe," Daniela said, tiredly reaching up to rub her temple. "None of it matters now though, does it? He's gone. I'm still here. I've got Sari, and life is good."

Another long silence came before her sister let out a slow, deep, modulated breath. "I guess it's probably a good thing you didn't tell me before," she said, "because I'm vibrating with so much anger right now that I probably would have killed him before he could kill himself."

Daniela laughed. "You think I didn't want to do the same? But I didn't because I knew his life would come to an end pretty quickly anyway. I did my best to understand what he was up to, but that got to be pretty hard too."

"You're a better person than I am," Davida said. "I wouldn't have stayed."

"No, but when I married, it was 'til death do us part, and I already knew that the death sentence had a termination date. Everybody could see he was failing rapidly. I would stick by my part of the bargain until his death. If he hadn't been terminal, I would have left."

"Are you okay now?"

"You mean, after his death or after the grocery store?"

A brittle laugh escaped her sister. "Both?"

"I'm fine," she said, suddenly very tired. "I'm heading home with Sari."

"And Sari's father?" Davida's voice changed, suddenly

becoming brisk. "Is he still here?"

"Not right now. He got a rental truck and is doing some work. I'm heading home from the store."

"Is he looking to move here?" Davida asked. "Are you sure you want to open that door?"

"That door was opened when he found out he was her father," Daniela said, not wanting to sit here and argue with her sister on this front too. "He's staying for a time to resolve a work issue at least."

"If he has a job, that's a plus," she said. "You should get some child support out of him."

Daniela snorted. "That is not why I contacted him."

"Maybe it should be," her sister said. "God knows you could use the money."

"That's got nothing to do with it. I'm doing fine, and you know it."

"Doesn't matter if you're doing fine or not. This guy has a job, and you're looking after his kid. Meanwhile he's getting off scot-free. That's not fair either."

"It's hardly scot-free," Daniela said. "He didn't even know Angel was pregnant, and he didn't find out about Sari until after she'd already been adopted."

"So he says," her sister snapped.

"Look. I can't deal with this right now," Daniela said. "I'll talk to you later."

With that, she hit the End Call button on her phone and tossed it into her purse. She'd listened to this conversation with her sister enough times to know that, for Davida, it always came back to money. Daniela knew it was concern on her sister's part, but that didn't make it any easier. Daniela would bend over backward to make sure Sari was fine, and she also was a little concerned about Angel being out there somewhere. It would be a whole lot easier if she wasn't. But then again, that was a horrible thought after having gone through Charlie's death.

She drove home, her mind consumed with her problems, but, when she finally pulled in, she realized just how exhausted she was. She climbed out, turned toward the back seat and saw Sari had fallen asleep in her car seat. Smiling, she grabbed the groceries and took them to the front door, then came right back and opened the truck's back door and unbuckled her little girl. Sari murmured but was limp as a dishrag, letting Daniela tuck her up against her heart as she carried her inside.

With the truck locked and the front door closed, she walked upstairs, where she laid the little girl down for her nap. When she was stretched out on the mattress, Daniela gently took off her little shoes and her coat and then tucked a blanket lightly around her. Back downstairs, she took the groceries to the kitchen and unpacked them. It was such a mundane chore, but it brought her a sense of peace. Settling into a routine was what she desperately needed. So much was going on in her life, but all she wanted was peace and quiet, along with a happy future for her and her daughter. Was that asking too much?

WESTON WASN'T SURE why he was back at the homestead, but, as soon as he'd gotten just a mile away from the wreck where Ginger and Grant had gone over the road, most likely with Shambhala, she started to bark again. He'd pulled off to the side of the road, trying to figure out what the problem was. When he turned to look at her, she went quiet again.

"What do you want to do, girl?"

Shambhala just looked at him. When he pulled into the road to turn around again, Shambhala started barking. He groaned.

"Okay, so does this mean you want to go back to the cabin?"

He felt foolish talking to the dog, as if expecting to get a straightforward answer, because nothing was straightforward about this. The dog was obviously lost and feeling like she was missing something special. But, if he could make the dog a little happier or more secure, it would be worth spending the time.

He drove back up to the cabin, and the dog whined to get out of the truck. He walked around and opened the door for her, then watched as the dog took off again, racing around the fields, then back up to the house, where she scratched on the front door. Weston walked up and opened the door, stepping inside.

It was a nice little homesteader cabin. He hoped the brother didn't sell it off too cheap because it was a nice place. He looked at some of the details he hadn't noticed before.

"Grant, did you do all this woodwork? If you did? Nice job, man." Indeed, a beautiful butcher block countertop was in the kitchen, and it was obvious a lot of time and love had gone into it. He opened a few drawers, looking to see if people had come in and cleaned out the place, but it was still fully stocked with dishes and cutlery in the utility drawer. He stopped when he saw a bunch of letters tossed on top. He pulled them out curiously.

"What was your life like, guys?" he murmured.

Shambhala went to the rug in front of the fireplace and lay down. That seemed to have been her spot.

He looked over at her, smiled and said, "You like that place, do you?"

Shambhala gave a heavy sigh and stretched out on her side.

That was the first time he realized she had dried blood on her underbelly as well. He frowned from a distance and then decided she should just stretch out and relax a bit, and he'd check it out later. After she was more comfortable around him.

As he studied her, he remembered the note in her file about loving music. He himself played the trumpet a bit, but had her adoptive family known about her favorite things? Living out here, they may not have indulged in a lot of electronics, especially if electricity was spotty out here. So maybe they wouldn't have played the radio constantly, nor had he seen any musical instruments. Right now she looked like she didn't have a care in the world.

Whatever the injury, it couldn't be too bad. She'd been very active since he'd gotten her, so she clearly wasn't hurting or slowing her down that he knew of. As he looked at the envelopes, he realized they were bills—one for truck insurance, and another one made his blood freeze.

Nothing was on the envelope except a single word. *Die.* He grabbed a set of tongs, flipped it over and realized the tongs would be useless because whoever had opened it had already put fingerprints all over it. But Weston wouldn't add any of his. Being as cautious as he could, he pulled out the letter with the tongs. It was a single piece of paper ripped off a notepad.

I told you to pay up, or you'll die. There was no signature. He laid it out on the kitchen counter and took several photos of it, then sent the pictures to the detective he'd spoken to earlier, Detective Kruger. Because, if you saw something like this, and then the people died, you have to wonder if something wasn't suspicious about the case. As soon as he sent the photo, he sent a text message. **Are you sure the deaths were accidental?**

He went through the rest of the mail but found nothing else suspicious. He put the rest of the mail back into the drawer. Then he did a quick search around the living room, looking for anything that might be out of the ordinary.

Shambhala hadn't seemed to be too bothered. She'd come in and gone straight to the fireplace, but that didn't mean that, with the cops having been in here, somebody else hadn't been as well. Weston searched the cupboards, high and low, and the bathroom, then went into the bedroom. Also a sleeping loft was upstairs, and, as he went up to see it, he found it was used more as a family den or sitting room with a great big soft couch for reading and lots of book-shelves stuffed full.

He wandered through the shelves, smiling when he saw the eclectic mix of fantasy, fiction and business books, right along with homesteading books. He shuffled some of the furniture around because it was light and easy to move, but nothing more was here to see.

He slowly made his way back down to the main part of the cabin, and, when he stepped into the first floor, it had a different sense to it. A different air about the room. He stepped back, looked around at the small house, wondering what it was he sensed, then took another step forward. He stopped in the doorway and just surveyed the structure. A log cabin with log outer walls, and the interior wall was some drywall on part of it and some tongue-and-groove on the other. It was an eclectic mix, again as if Grant had done some of his own work after-the-fact.

A small bathroom was attached. He wandered through it again, back to the bedroom, wondering what it was about the room that bothered him.

Then he realized only one pillow was on the bed. He made note of that and walked over to the closets, checking to see if it was still full of both sets of clothing. He opened up the doors to see only men's clothing. He frowned at that. Just as he was sorting it out, his phone rang. It was the detective.

"Where did you find that?" the detective asked harshly.

"I'm in the cabin now. That envelope was in the utility drawer with other mail. And, yes, it was open already."

"And now you've got your fingerprints all over it too, I suppose."

"No, I used a pair of tongs," he said. "I wasn't born yesterday. I'll be happy to put it in a bag and bring it in to you."

"I'm on my way out there," the detective said. "I had to come out that direction anyway."

"Yeah, and maybe you could tell me why no women's clothing is in the closet." There was an odd silence. "There should be, shouldn't there? Did the brother come up here after all?"

"Not that I know of," the detective said. "I've spoken to him on the phone, but he didn't say anything about coming."

"The closet is empty of female clothing. And only one pillow is on the bed."

"I'll contact him and see if he did then."

"Otherwise, who's had access?"

"I can't tell you that, but, if people know they're dead and gone, it's possible a squatter has moved in."

"It's possible." Weston turned as he hit the End Call button on the phone and caught sight of movement.

Instinctively he dropped to his knees, then turned as a blow came out of nowhere. It was enough to shake him but not stun him. He reached out with his right fist, connecting with a jawbone. The man went to his knees, and Weston followed up with a hard left and dropped him.

Shambhala stood in the doorway, whining.

He looked over at her, surprised. "Come here, girl," he said. She came forward, wagging her tail, but obviously upset. He looked down at the man on the ground. "So, do you know who this is?"

She whined, but she didn't bark at the intruder.

Weston picked up the man in a fireman's carry and took him to the kitchen, where Weston propped his captive up on a chair at the kitchen table and tied his legs together. For all Weston knew, *he* was the intruder and not this guy. He went over in his mind the first few minutes that he'd been in the house, but there'd been no sign of anyone. There'd been no call out or anything. And Shambhala hadn't acted surprised. That was the odd part of this.

While the guy was unconscious, Weston went through his pockets and came up with a name that made him stop. This guy was Grant Buckman. As in, the man who lived here.

Weston frowned. The guy carried credit cards in his name too. Weston went through the rest of the wallet. The guy had a cell phone in his other pocket. He took several photos of the Contacts list and checked most of the texts from the last couple weeks. Apparently Grant had been gone for six weeks.

So, what the hell was going on here? The guy was just

starting to wake up when Weston heard the sound of a vehicle coming up the driveway. Keeping his eye on Grant or whoever this guy was, Weston opened the front door as the detective hopped out of his vehicle.

"You got that letter for me?" the detective asked.

"Yeah, but we've got bigger problems than that."

"What's up?" The detective stepped inside, took one look at the prisoner tied to the chair and gasped.

"I don't know what the hell's going on here," Weston said, "but, according to his ID and credit cards, this is Grant Buckman. And, if this is Grant, who in the hell got buried along with Ginger?"

CHAPTER 7

D ANIELA SET OUT all the prep work for dinner, but she wasn't sure when Weston would make it home. She checked her phone several times to see if he'd texted her, but she found no message. Sari was enjoying building with her blocks and playing with her dolls. She had this peculiar habit of creating little monuments and having her dolly sit right beside them. She wondered if she'd seen a lot of people taking selfies or something. It wasn't something Daniela did, but she'd certainly seen enough other people taking photos of themselves all the time. Maybe so did Sari.

Keeping busy with cleaning had been Daniela's strategy this afternoon in order to avoid rehashing the conversation she'd had at the grocery store earlier. Finally she sat beside her computer with a heavy *thud*. Daniela looked over at Sari, who was completely oblivious and happily getting her dolls to build blocks. Daniela smiled at the innocence of the little girl at eighteen months old. She wasn't a baby but wasn't quite a toddler yet either. She walked and talked and garbled sentences, but she wasn't superclear on her diction yet.

Daniela looked around at the kitchen in the house she rented, wishing she had a nice home of her own. But, when her husband got ill, they hadn't had enough money for the medical bills, so they ended up selling their home and getting this rental. It seemed like everything she had done and sacrificed had been to keep him in good health. The fact that he'd repaid her the way he had was something that still burned.

She couldn't be upset with her sister because Davida was just concerned about her. Yet Davida didn't understand how her attitude just made life harder on everybody.

Enough of trying to distract herself. Daniela opened her laptop. She was due to go to work in two days, but she was a temporary employee doing part-time work and always had to be checking on her shifts. Sure enough, her shift had been canceled. That was both good and bad right now. She needed the time with Weston, but it meant a smaller paycheck. She was building a sideline business with an online store, like an Etsy, but not quite. She was looking at the big vendors, trying to see if she could do something like that, but she was running a tea shop, growing her own tea herbs. It was small and fairly minor, more of a hobby than anything really successful. But it was something that made her smile. Something that put a sense of pride back into her spine. Maybe down the road she'd do more with it, but, right now, it was all about putting food on the table and keeping a roof over their heads. The last thing she wanted was any more of this emotional upset.

When she opened up her email, she realized how unlikely that last thought would be because she found an email from Angel. Daniela shut her eyes, just at seeing the name. Forcing herself to click on it and open it, she read the short missive with horror. *Hope Sari's well. I'd like to come see her. I miss her and want her in my life. Maybe permanently.*

And that was it. But the fact that Angel had even contacted her and then said she wanted Sari in her life was terrifying. They were both things Daniela didn't want to deal with. But the phrase, *maybe permanently*, that undid her. She glanced at Sari, feeling her heart tighten, as if somebody had squeezed all the life out of it. She could barely catch her breath.

Sitting back from the laptop, she looked at her shaking fingers, clenching them into fists. She wanted to run across the room and snatch up her daughter and race to the other side of the world, where no one would ever find her. Even if she picked her up gently, Daniela would surely hug her daughter so tight that she would frighten Sari, and yet it still wouldn't be enough for Daniela. She wanted to absorb her daughter into her very essence, so she could never lose her. Because Angel came with that threat of loss. Threat that the birth mother would try to take her daughter back again. Daniela didn't know where she stood on that legally.

They had a contract and paperwork, saying she had adopted Sari, but almost any judge would have to consider the birth mother's request to get back into her daughter's life, and it didn't seem to matter what Daniela wanted. Or what was best for Sari. It wasn't fair.

As she sat here shaking, her phone rang. Afraid it was Angel, she didn't want to even look at it. When it didn't stop, she finally nudged her phone and saw it was Weston. She snatched up the phone. "Hello?"

"What's wrong?" Weston asked, his voice instantly alert. "Are you okay? Is the baby okay?"

She took a deep, slow breath. "We're both fine," she said. "Sorry, your call surprised me."

"That didn't sound like surprise," he said, not giving an inch.

She shook her head. "I'm fine. I'll tell you about it when you get home."

"Fine," he said, "but we need to get to the bottom of it."

"Why?" she asked. "What's happened?"

"A lot of things have happened, but I haven't figured it out yet. I'm just calling to say I won't be home probably for at least an hour and a half."

She checked the clock. "Okay, it's about four now, so we can tentatively plan dinner for six*ish*, if that works for you. I'm sorry but I forgot to pick up steaks for dinner."

"That's fine," he said. "But I don't know if I'll make it to the grocery store to pick them up either."

She laughed. "If you'll be late, then chicken breasts would be easier."

"I'd rather have a steak," he said with a more amused tone, "but we can have that tomorrow night. Anyway, I'm just checking in," he said, then he hung up.

She stared down at the phone with a smile. "Maybe you were *just* checking in, but it's nice nonetheless," she murmured. And it was nice. Nice to know somebody out there cared enough to let her know when he was coming. And who she cared enough about to be thrilled to know he was staying until tomorrow.

She didn't have a relationship with him, not in the way most people defined a relationship, but she really liked the man. Something was just so damn special about him. His bond to Sari made her pause and worry, but she didn't want to go there. No, all any of it did was emphasize how lonely Daniela was, and how lonely she'd been for a very long time. Sari filled the gaping wound in her heart, but a child wasn't a substitute for an adult relationship.

Daniela hadn't even considered moving forward with another relationship in the past year, though certainly men had been interested. Even though she still wore her wedding ring in an attempt to keep most men away.

But Sari had come first. And now somehow Sari's father had made himself a spot in her home as well. Sure, she'd asked him to come into Sari's life, but somehow she hadn't really realized that coming into Sari's life also meant coming into hers as well. It had seemed so completely normal and natural that he would check in and let her know when he would be back, so she would know how to plan for dinner. Even still, she was checking her phone all the time to see if anything new came from him.

She shook her head. "It's time for …" she announced, as she hopped to her feet and walked into the kitchen.

"Tea?" Sari called, as she toddled behind her.

Daniela looked down at her sweet baby. "How about milk for you?" Daniela reached down and scooped her up, setting her in the special little chair at the table, and poured her a sippy cup of milk, giving her something to enjoy. She quickly put the teakettle on for herself.

She was a great connoisseur of teas of all kinds, from black to green to many herb concoctions. Those were what she grew and sold on her website. As she made herself a cup of tea, she sat here, wishing she could grow and brew the other missing parts of her life. A cup of tea was a cup of comfort, but it was a small bandage over a much bigger issue. She sat down with a heavy sigh, then picked up her warm cup of tea and smiled at her daughter. "Not to worry, sweetheart. We'll be just fine."

Sari looked up at her and cried out, "Doggy, doggy."

Daniela laughed. "He's coming back too. Both of them."

THEIR PRISONER WASN'T cooperating. It had taken a while to get him conscious, and, once he realized he was tied up and facing the deputy now too, he'd gotten very still. When he realized the cops had his wallet, he buttoned his lip and hadn't said a word.

Weston looked at the detective. "Do you know him?"

"No."

"Do we know anybody who did? This is either Grant or it's somebody impersonating him, and, if so, where the hell did he get his wallet?"

The detective nodded, walked a few feet away and pulled out his phone to make a call.

Weston was hoping to listen in, but the detective had stepped out on the front porch. Weston sat down across from the man. "Dude, if this is your house, speak up. I'm the intruder here, if that's the case. But since we're trying to solve what happened to Ginger and Grant, who died when they went off the road, we're a little confused as to who you are and why you are carrying Grant's ID."

The man just glared at him.

With a sudden thought, Weston got up and looked around at the photos in the house and brought one back. It showed the couple. He held it up against the man's face and frowned.

"It could be you. But, if you are Grant, why wouldn't you say something?"

The man still didn't say a word.

Weston looked over at Shambhala, who was lying in front of the fireplace. She came to attention when the detective arrived, but she hadn't growled or barked. And she seemed to be perfectly comfortable with this guy. If it was Grant, then, of course, she'd be comfortable. But, if that was the case, why hadn't he brought the dog home with him, six weeks ago? "No excuse leaving the dog to suffer on her own," he announced.

The stranger's eyebrows shot up. He glanced over at the dog and frowned. Shambhala didn't seem to care one way or another.

"She either knows you really well," Weston said, "or she doesn't see you as a particular threat."

At that, the corner of the man's lips turned down, but he still didn't speak.

Weston shrugged. "Well, you're not going anywhere for a long time anyway."

"You can't hold me here," the man said. "I haven't done anything wrong."

"You're squatting inside someone else's house," Weston informed him. "That's the least of it. If you've assumed another man's identity, then that's a whole different story as well." Weston could see the other guy hesitating. "And, if you are Grant, you have a hell of a pile of explaining to do."

The guy resumed glaring at him again.

The detective returned. "According to the photos from police files, he's looking like Grant. But, if he's Grant, what the hell is going on?"

"Exactly. And I agree he does look like Grant." Weston held up the photo he'd taken off the wall.

The detective looked at it and nodded. "We have something similar."

"So, is it Grant? Do you have any mention of Grant having a family in your police files?"

"Just his brother, Gregory," the detective said.

"Did anybody mention they were twins?"

The detective's eyebrows shot up, and he frowned. "Are

you Gregory then?" he asked the guy.

The man's eyes went from one to the other, and his shoulders all of a sudden sagged. "I'm Grant."

"So says you," said Weston. "Now I don't believe you."

The man glared at him. "I'm in my home. I've got my ID, and you can see from the photos it's me."

"No, not necessarily," the detective said. "I've also got a dead man, buried and gone, who was ID'd as Grant. I spoke to a brother who was coming up here."

Grant said. "You spoke to me."

"No, not buying it," Weston said. "If this was your house, you would have kicked me out. You wouldn't have let us in, and you wouldn't have hidden like you did. So the only reason you're still hiding, if you are Grant, is if you had something to do with your wife's death, as well as the man who was with her."

"It was her lover," he said bitterly. "And that lover was my brother."

"Whoa, whoa, whoa. Hang on a minute." The detective held his hands up by his shoulders. "So was it you I talked to or your brother?"

"There's just the two of us, and it was me you talked to," he said, as if he was suddenly tired of the whole mess. "My wife and her lover were killed, so I moved back into my house. But I knew it would look bizarre, and, once I realized you had identified him as me, I laid low over these past several weeks, trying to figure out what I should do about it. There are some advantages to dying and disappearing," he said. "I could go down and take up my brother's life. Or I could wipe him off the face of the earth too," he said with a shrug. "I hadn't figured it out yet."

"Six weeks is a long time to figure it out," Weston said.

He looked back at the dog, who was now sleeping in front of the fireplace. "Why didn't the dog come and greet you?"

"She greeted me on the other side of the house," he said. "And then, when I came in, I just ordered her to go lie down, so she did."

"That makes sense," Weston said. "So why didn't you go find the dog after she went missing in the accident?"

"How was I supposed to know where she was?" he exclaimed. "The truck went off the road, and I never heard any more. The dog was gone. My wife was dead, and so was my brother."

"So, what you're trying to decide is which one of you had more money? Then you would assume that life?"

"Not really," he said, "I inherit anyway."

"So, does your disappearance and trying to figure out which person you should pop back up as have something to do with that threatening letter?"

The guy blanched. "What do you know about the letter?"

"I found it," Weston said. "We were looking into the accident, thinking the letter was about you, and I still don't have any reason to change my way of thinking."

"It wasn't for me. It was for him, and I think the threatening letter was for real," he said. "That's another reason why I was trying to figure out which way to work this. If I'm alive, and they know it, then they'll come after me again."

"You mean, that's the real reason why you've been hiding out here," Weston said. "After they killed your wife and your brother accidentally, you figured you were safe, but only if nobody knew you were alive."

Grant nodded. "Something like that, yes. And my brother would have come up to see me if I had died anyway."

"Would he though?"

"If I had died and left my wife alone, yes. As it was, I was gone on a trip for quite a while, and he came anyway." At that, the same bitter note could be heard in his voice.

"Did you know they were carrying on behind your back?"

"No," he said, "I didn't. But then again my brother and I look a lot alike. And I'm not sure, if my brother stepped into my shoes, if my wife knew or not."

At that, the two men stopped and stared at him.

"You're thinking your wife didn't know it was your brother and not you?"

"No, I'm not sure she did," he repeated. "When I came back, I stepped into the kitchen, and she ripped into me because I was supposed to have done something that morning and hadn't. I just stopped her and said, 'Whoa, hang on a minute there,' and she wouldn't. She just kept yelling at me. I stepped back out, not sure what I was supposed to do, when I realized my brother was driving in with his vehicle. I hauled him off to the shed, where I beat the crap out of him. Then he admitted he'd come in for a visit, and she'd thrown her arms around him, pretty hot and heavy, and he had succumbed to temptation."

Weston stared at him.

Grant nodded grimly. "What the hell was I supposed to do then? At that point, I looked pretty stupid, but, then again, my wife would look bad as well. My asshole of a brother should have identified himself."

"Your wife didn't know?"

"I don't know," he said tiredly. "But, when the vehicle went off the road, it wasn't me. It was him. I'd been trying to deal with how to get back into her life as it was."

"Hang on a minute. How long were you gone for?"

"I was gone for three weeks, working at a mine, back for one, then gone for another four," he said. "I was working up north. I saw the letter the first time I was here. I put it away in the drawer, not sure what to do about it. Then I was gone for the last four weeks and came back just before the accident. That's when my wife reamed me out, and my brother and I had the big toss-up over it all. The next thing I know, they're both heading out in the truck, and I never saw either of them again."

"And where was Shambhala at this time?"

He looked at Weston in surprise. "I have no clue. Why?"

"Was the dog in the back of the truck?"

He thought about it for a moment, then shrugged. "She must have been. She wasn't here. After they left, I came back into the cabin, determined to move back into my own house and have it out with them. That's when I found out my wife was pregnant. She'd left a pregnancy test on the counter. And it was positive. Only I knew chances were, it wasn't mine. It was my brother's."

The three men sat for a long moment in silence.

"Jesus," Weston said. "If your brother did all that without you knowing, and without her knowing, that's even shittier than—I don't know. I'm at a loss."

"It was the worst of the worst," Grant admitted. "The thing is, I'm also not sure if that letter was for me or for him."

"Why would you think that?"

"Because I've never done anything wrong," he said. "I've been sitting here, trying to figure out what happened to my life. My pregnant wife just ended up dead. My brother is gone, and this threatening letter, which came while I was away, makes no sense to me. But, for all I know, that's the reason why they are dead."

"Okay, this is really confusing," the detective said. "You don't have any clue who sent that threatening letter, nor really to whom?"

"No," Grant said, "I don't. I know that's confusing. That's why I've been lying low, trying to figure out what the hell I'm supposed to do."

"Jesus Christ," Weston said.

At that time, the dog hopped up from her nap and walked closer to them. Instead of going to Grant, she went to Weston. Weston gently stroked her head and scratched her behind the ears.

"Every time she comes close," Weston said, looking at Grant, "she comes to me, not to you."

"I know," he said, "but I've been gone a lot. Shambhala was more my wife's dog than mine."

"You think?" the detective asked in a sour tone.

But Weston could understand Kruger's point and his sour disposition too. A ton of paperwork had to be dealt with, all because of the duplicity of this man in front of them and then that of his twin brother. The authorities would likely have to exhume the body and verify who they had buried. "It's also quite possible," Weston said, "that you are Gregory, trying, for some perverted reason, to step into Grant's life."

The detective nodded. "Do you have any idea what a nightmare this is for the police department?"

"You do what you have to do," Grant said, his face suddenly losing all vitality. "Just remember. Not very long ago I was a happily married man with my future ahead of me, and now apparently my brother, my wife and what? A baby—my son or daughter, or my nephew or niece, I guess—they're all gone. So, if you think it's confusing and inconvenient for you, just imagine how I feel. I'm so conflicted. I'm angry, hurt and grieving for everybody involved. It's just devastating."

"But you're not an animal person, are you?"

"What does that have to do with anything?" Grant asked in frustration.

Weston shrugged. "Not a lot, I guess. It's just odd because you've got an animal here that desperately needed care, and yet you weren't giving it to her."

"But remember," Grant said. "I didn't know what happened to the dog."

"And yet I can't imagine the dog, if it was in the back of that vehicle right up to the crash, having gone anywhere but back home again," Weston said, stating a truth that was hard for anybody to argue.

"Well, if she did," Grant said, "maybe one of the rescuers took her back into town, and she ended up running away."

"That's possible," Weston said, nodding his head slowly.

"Thank you," he said. "I know you're thinking I'm involved in something shady, and I am—but it's not by choice. I didn't do anything to deserve this."

"Not sure that blame or what you deserve has any place in this," the detective said. "This is just shit from start to finish."

Grant nodded. "Finally you've said something that makes sense, but you still don't get it. You might have paperwork to catch up on, and you might have a dog to deal with, but I've lost everything."

CHAPTER 8

D ANIELA WATCHED AS the truck drove up the long driveway to her small house. She stepped out onto the porch, with Sari in her arms, and watched Shambhala jump out of the truck, shaking herself as she hit the ground, then running up the few steps toward them. Her missing leg didn't seem to affect her or to slow her down. In her arms, Sari started to wiggle and clap her hands.

"Doggy, doggy!"

Daniela crouched in front of Shambhala, who started to clean Sari's face. Laughing and crying out, Sari tried to grab the dog's head, but her pudgy fingers and the dog's cheeks started slipping past each other. The dog darted in for kisses and then left again.

When Daniela straightened up, Weston stood there with his hands on his hips, looking at the three of them. She smiled. "It doesn't look like you had a good afternoon."

"Definitely an odd one," he said, providing a somewhat cryptic answer. "Sometimes you just never know how things will turn out."

"Well, that's confusing," she said, as she turned and walked back inside.

"Very confusing," he said. He lifted his head and sniffed. "Smells great."

"Let's hope it tastes great too. Dinner's ready," she said,

checking the clock on the kitchen wall. "Or it will be in a few minutes, if you want to go wash up."

He took the hint and nodded, heading down the hallway to the bathroom.

She put Sari in her high chair. "It's time for food."

Sari laughed. "Doggy eat too."

Daniela remembered the dog food they had bought at the feedstore and realized it was still in the back of her truck. "Let's hope Weston can get it for us," she said with a smile.

"Go get what?" Weston asked, as he walked back into the kitchen.

"The dog food for Shambhala. It's still in my truck."

He nodded. "I'm on it." And headed out the front door. Minutes later he came back in with a large bag on his shoulder.

She looked at it in surprise. "It didn't look nearly that big in the store."

"Do you have a bowl I can use?"

Smiling, she pulled out two bowls—one for food and one for water. She gave him the one for food and filled the other with water. Together they placed the dishes down where the dog could eat in peace. Shambhala came over, tail wagging, and dug into the food.

"I wonder when she had her last meal."

"A handful of treats at the feedstore would be my guess," he said with a laugh. "Best not to have Sari get close to Shambhala when she's eating. Clearly she's been suffering for some time, and she might be possessive over food for a while."

"It's so terrible she lost her owners."

"You don't know the half of it."

"Oh?" she asked.

He nodded. "I'll tell you over dinner."

She served up three plates, and, as he sat down, she asked, "So, what happened this afternoon?"

"What happened was," he said, "we found a man in Grant and Ginger's cabin, or rather I found one when he attacked me. But he claims to be Grant and says the guy who died in the accident with Ginger was his twin brother." And then he gave her the details.

She ended up putting down her knife and fork, interrupting her dinner. "Seriously? The brother stepped into Grant's life while he was away at work, and the wife didn't know? Is that possible?"

"That's what Grant says anyway. And maybe he's just hoping that's the way it was, that his wife and brother weren't just carrying on behind his back all this time."

She winced at that. "If so, that's really disgusting, and honestly I'm not sure I could believe the wife wouldn't have known it wasn't him."

He looked up at her for a long moment. "Do you think you could tell the twins apart?"

"As the wife, absolutely," she said. "Everything would be different, you know? From the different clothing, different mannerisms, different smells, a different way of making love. They might look the same, but the men themselves would be very different."

"Well, that was my opinion too," Weston said, "so maybe Grant is delusional and is just hoping it's that way. Otherwise, he has to accept they were carrying on behind his back."

"And then you have to wonder if he isn't the one who killed them," she said. "If anybody killed them of course. But if you found out your brother was carrying on with your wife, and she was now pregnant with probably your brother's child, what would you do?"

"What I would do and what I'd be tempted to do," he said, "are two different things. But you're right. Anyone would definitely be tempted to send them both over a cliff on a permanent basis."

NOT ONLY HAD Daniela given him something to think about, Weston now had a different issue at hand as well. He stepped out the kitchen back door onto the patio and sent Badger an update. When Badger called a few minutes later, Weston wasn't surprised.

Badger said incredulously, "Is it really a mix-up of identities between two brothers?"

"I'm not sure," Weston said honestly. "When you think about it, it could go either way. The threatening letter does add some validity for Grant wanting to hide his identity."

"But it also potentially gives Gregory, who may have thought about stepping into his brother's shoes, a chance to reverse course, so he's not who he started out to be."

It took Weston a moment to figure that out, but then he could see Badger's point. "Right, so you got a shitty scenario either way. Whether the dead guy is Gregory or Grant, the writer of the threatening letter may realize maybe the wrong brother was murdered, and, if the bad guys find out the other brother's still alive, the bad guys may realize they got the wrong guy and come after whoever is left alive."

"Exactly."

"Then why would this brother hang around?" Weston asked. "What could be the reason for staying?"

"Maybe to see if something can be done? Maybe to see if the property has any value? It's a homestead up there with a house on it. Depends on what kind of lifestyle he wants. What we need to do is find out if either of the brothers were in each other's will."

"The local police are on that," said Weston. "And the problem is, none of this really has to do with Shambhala. She was supposedly in the back of the truck, but yet nobody saw her there, and nobody saw her at home. I caught her near the local feedstore."

"Yeah, that's another mystery," Badger said. "And you're right. That's our priority. We need to find a home for her, where she'll be safe and content."

"She also didn't react with this guy when we talked to him," Weston said. "Not happy or negative."

"Which, for a dog like that, is very odd," Badger said with frustration in his voice.

"I know," Weston said. "It's all a bit on the bizarre side."

"You want to check around and see if there are any potential places where we can foster the dog?" Badger asked. "And what's your time commitment to this project? Do you want to come back immediately, or are you okay to stay for a week or two?"

An odd note was in Badger's voice, and Weston realized he was really asking about the scenario with his daughter. "I'm currently staying with my daughter's mother." He realized how bizarre that sounded. "My daughter took one look at me and started bawling," he said with a laugh. "On the other hand, she took one look at Shambhala and fell in love."

"And is that a good place for Shambhala?" Badger asked curiously. "Can her mother handle a dog like that?"

"I'm not sure, to be honest," he said. "She doesn't have a whole lot of money, and she's renting."

"Okay," Badger said slowly. "No offense intended here, but is she the kind who would look after the dog?"

"I believe she is the kind, Badger," Weston said slowly. "But it's a huge commitment. Shambhala's only four, so there's easily five to ten years left in her life, or more."

"True enough," Badger said. After a moment of silence he added, "Give me some time to think about our options here."

"On any of the other cases, did you have to find a foster home?"

"No," Badger said in surprise. "This is the first one we've come up against."

Weston frowned. It made him feel like he had failed at his job somehow. "What happened to the dogs?"

"Depending on the circumstances, a lot of the guys kept them," Badger said honestly. "And in Pete Lowery's case, well, his dog had been taken from his care because he had to go into a VA home and couldn't have the dog with him. So, at that point, the job to reunite Pete and his dog was our primary goal, not to mention Pete was perfectly capable of living at home by then, but he had a greedy brother involved."

"The little bastard," Weston said in an amiable voice. "We keep seeing the dark side of humanity at every corner, don't we?"

"Yes, we do," Badger said. "But good men are out there, period. Anyway, give me some time to think about this. And, if you have more updates on the two brothers, let me know."

After he rang off, Weston remained outside on the patio, while Shambhala lay in the yard. She seemed perfectly content. But then, she'd been perfectly content to be at the fireplace back at the cabin today too. He wondered if the paperwork for her was in Ginger's name or Grant's because ownership of the dog might become an issue. In that case, he may not even be able to take Shambhala to another foster home for care. He sent Badger a text, asking that question. Badger came back saying the dog had been signed over to Ginger.

Interesting. Because that wasn't the same thing as Grant saying he was willing and capable of looking after the dog. So the push for the dog had been Ginger's, and maybe that was why Shambhala was doing better here because of the presence of the two females. Maybe Shambhala's history so far hadn't left her too much faith in men. She'd had good training but had lost her trainer. That was a circumstance Weston didn't know the details of. But, just like in any case, history was important.

He sent another text to Badger, asking about the fate of Shambhala's trainer. He replied a few minutes later.

Trainers actually. Like so many of the K9, they are dedicated to just one man at a time. When a trainer leaves the military service, or goes into a different department, he often has to relinquish the dog, who is an asset of the US government. In this case Shambhala was relinquished to another man and then went through a series of different trainers as they taught her new techniques that they could then impart to other dogs. That's when she ended up in a bombing incident, and the decision was made to retire her.

Her injuries don't appear to bother her too much, Weston responded.

Good. She's done her duty by all of us, and what she needs now is a few good years where she can just relax

and have a good life.

Weston left it at that.

He walked across the grass toward her. Shambhala just watched him, her gaze steady. But there was no fear, just observation. He crouched in front of her. Reaching out, he stroked and scratched the dog. Her missing leg appeared to be inconsequential to her. He noted she had jumped in and out of the truck without any issues, though it might become a bigger problem as she got older.

Shambhala rolled over on her back and gave him her belly. He gently stroked her and gave her a really good belly rub. Thankfully the dried blood was gone. He could see a small scab over a scratch, but it appeared to be a minor injury. Same thing when he checked out her haunch. That was good. He just wanted to impart friendliness, cooperation and, of course, build a bond with her.

At that last bit his mind stuttered to a stop, surprised he wanted to bond with this dog. Was it fair to build a bond and then have her go to somebody else? How happy had she been with Ginger? Shambhala had appeared to have been very relaxed, if not bonded to Ginger, as Shambhala had gone straight to the carpet in front of the cabin's fireplace, as if that was her go-to comfort zone. But that didn't mean she had the same comfort with her owners as she'd had with her trainers.

A lot of dogs just detached after a while. They said that a dog would always find somebody new to bond with, but, after so many different people, dogs did tend to get a little more detached, and it would take longer to bond each time.

Just then the patio doors opened behind him. Daniela and Sari stepped out, Sari holding her mom's hand as she made her way awkwardly down the steps. But no doubt about where she was headed. She had her free arm forward, reaching for Shambhala.

"Doggy, doggy."

Daniela laughed. "We're getting there."

He watched as Shambhala lifted her head and wagged her tail as she saw the two women coming toward her. Whereas Weston himself hadn't been given a tail wag, not the happy kind here. Instinctively he knew it was logical, but he had to admit to feeling let down. He'd always had a good rapport with animals. He was up against some history here, and he didn't know how to deal with it.

As Sari got closer, she tumbled and fell to her knees. Instinctively Weston jumped forward to make sure the dog wouldn't hurt her, but instead Shambhala reached up and licked Sari's face. Sari laughed, then fell forward on top of Shambhala's belly. Daniela tried to pull her back but lost her grip on the little fingers. She turned to look back at him and frowned. "Do you think this is safe?"

He walked over to Shambhala, who was even now lying there blissfully happy as Sari reached up to pet her, which ended up being more like a smack on the face.

"I can't honestly say," he said. "But, if Shambhala is bonding with anybody, I'd say it's with Sari."

At that moment, Shambhala rolled over slightly, knocking Sari to the grass, and she stared up at him with surprise and then laughed. Shambhala licked her face again. Then the two of them just curled up, intertwined. Shambhala sat in between Sari's legs, her chubby little arm wrapped around the dog's neck, their heads together.

He caught the sound of Daniela's breath quickly sucked back. He pulled out his phone and started taking pictures.

CHAPTER 9

"**A**RE YOU TAKING pictures because it's cute," Daniela said in a faint voice, "or because this is dangerous?"

"I've been around pets all my life," he said. "Nothing in Shambhala's body language says she's dangerous."

"I know," she said, "but how quickly will Shambhala switch from this to a guard dog?"

He looked at her and smiled. "Well, if she switches to a guard dog, you'd be blessed," he said, "because she would protect Sari with her life."

She looked at him, surprised, then looked down at Sari and Shambhala. "Well, good. It's perfect timing."

"What's that?"

She let out her breath and slowly tried to get calm. "Because Angel contacted me today. Via email. And if there's one thing I don't trust, it's that woman." She hadn't meant to say it that way, and, after his look, she shrugged and nodded. "I was going to tell you earlier, but I forgot, what with all the things you had on your mind."

"We did have a lot of other stuff to talk about." He glanced again at Sari and frowned. "Do you have legal documents giving you custody of Sari?"

"I do," she said, "but you also know that, in some cases, particularly something like this, one where it didn't go through a government agency, the judges do tend to favor the birth parents."

"Ah," he said, "so you really are worried Angel is after Sari now?"

"You would be too if you saw the email she sent." She pulled out her phone, found Angel's email and handed it to him.

"Do you really think, if you say no, she'll come and steal her away?"

"I think it's a strong possibility. I don't know what to say, other than that, because it's obviously my ... my biggest fear."

He nodded. "I can see that." He crossed his arms, tapping his finger on his forearm.

"What do you think?"

"I'm thinking Shambhala would quite likely protect Sari, if that were the case. But I'm not sure you're prepared to handle the cost and the commitment required to deal with a dog like this."

"It sounds like a huge responsibility," she said. "And that would be very difficult for me. Money aside, the dog will need training, I presume."

He looked at her, and the corner of his mouth tilted upward. "Not quite. You'd be the one who needs training."

She looked at him, startled for a moment, then glanced back at the dog lying there, completely happy as Sari lay on top of her, happily chattering away, telling her some story. Sari's head was against Shambhala's ear, which twitched with every breath.

"Shambhala looks so gentle right now," Daniela murmured. "It's hard to believe she'd be anything other than this."

"I do know from her training," Weston said, "that she

can be a whole lot more than this experience, but she is retired. I don't know what her last six weeks were like. I don't even know what her last six months were like. But the training she would have gone through originally would have been rigorous, intensive and ongoing."

"I need to learn more than basic commands," she said, "but right now she looks like nothing but a teddy bear."

Privately he had to agree. He stepped back to see if Shambhala would react differently. But she appeared to be happy. He took several more steps back.

Daniela looked at him sharply. "Are you trying to do that?"

He nodded. "Take several steps back too, please." She hesitated. He looked at her with a smile. "I would never endanger Sari."

She took several more steps back, so they were both about eight feet away from the dog. Shambhala didn't even open her eyes.

"So, is this a good thing or a bad thing?" Daniela asked with a laugh, as she joined Weston farther away from the dog.

"It looks like her focus is on Sari," he said quietly. "I don't know what would happen if somebody came up and disturbed them."

"And I don't want to find out."

He smiled. "How long do you want to leave Sari out here?"

"I hate to take her away," she admitted. "She doesn't have a lot of playmates around here. Plus I think she just adopted Shambhala."

"That may be," he said, "but that doesn't necessarily mean it's the right decision to keep the dog. If we even were to get that cleared."

Daniela walked toward her daughter. "Come on, Sari. Do you want to play in the sandbox?"

Sari turned to look at her and asked, "Doggy come?"

Daniela hesitated.

Weston asked, "Where's the sandbox?"

"At the park around the corner. It's got a pretty decent-size sandbox."

"Why don't we all go," he said. "It will give me a chance to see what Shambhala's training is like."

"That's a good idea." Daniela smiled down at Sari. "Yes. We'll take Shambhala to the park."

Sari squeezed Shambhala and scrambled to her feet, toddling unsteadily toward her mother.

"Doggy, come," she ordered in a strict tone, directed at the dog. It was so funny to see her voice change as she tried to be an adult, as she tried to mimic Weston's command.

Weston walked closer to Sari, crouched and said, "When you want the doggy to do something, you look at her in her good eye, reach out with your arm and make this motion, and then you give her the order to come."

Sari stared at him with her huge eyes, looked back at Shambhala and moved her hand the way she was supposed to and said, "Doggy, come."

Shambhala looked at Weston and looked at the little girl. Then, with her tongue lolling to the side, she hopped to her feet and went over to Sari. As she arrived, she gave Sari another lick on the face.

Sari laughed, hanging on to the dog for support, as they walked back toward the stairs. Daniela watched closely, completely flabbergasted that the dog would follow the little girl's commands, but Shambhala seemed to realize she was needed for steadiness. As they went up the steps, she took them at the exact same pace as Sari.

"She's so good with Sari," she said in wonder.

"I see that. So let's take this chance to put Shambhala through her paces, see what else she might know." With the leash once again attached to her collar, Shambhala hesitated at the door. But when she saw everybody else was getting boots on and walking out the door along with her, she seemed to be totally okay.

"Did you see that? I'm not sure she would be happy to leave without you," he murmured.

"I don't think it's *without me*," Daniela said. "It's *without Sari.*"

"True enough."

As they wandered down the lane toward the park, Sari was busy stomping in recent puddles and then picking up rocks, trying to hand them to Shambhala, who would sniff them and keep walking. Weston kept an eye on Shambhala, who appeared to be keeping an eye on Sari. "For whatever reason," he said, "she's in protective mode over Sari."

"I won't argue against it," Daniela said. "I just don't know how to turn it on and off."

"There may be no Off button in this case because I don't think she's doing this by command. I think she's doing this because she wants to."

"Meaning that she cares about Sari?"

"She definitely cares about Sari. A strong bond exists already between them."

At that, Daniela shook her head. "I don't know that I'm ready for the commitment to keep a dog, any dog really," she said. "And I can't even imagine trying to feed her."

"Not a discussion for today, that's for sure."

"Well, if it doesn't fit in today," she challenged, "when does it? Because, as far as I know, you're leaving tomorrow." She watched him carefully as he hesitated, then looked at her and smiled.

"How would you feel about a houseguest for a week or two?"

WESTON WATCHED A pretty smile bloom across her face. Then he gave a nod. "Only if you're okay with it. I do want to sort out the Grant, Gregory and Ginger thing, and I do need to make sure Shambhala has a foster home, stays with me or stays with you."

She hesitated at that and looked down.

He grabbed her hand and squeezed it gently. "No pressure, Daniela. Really."

She gave a light laugh. "So good to hear that, because you know something, Weston? As much as I'm okay with keeping Shambhala, I'm not flush with money."

"I get that. It sounds like we need to deal with Angel too."

"Yes, we do," she said sadly.

"Do you think she just wants to have regular visits with Sari?"

"I don't know. Am I a bad person for not even wanting her to have that? She would be a horrible influence with her lifestyle."

"I think the hardest thing for a child is a parent who flips in and out on a whim," he said. "Are you looking at me for the same problem?"

She just shrugged, not saying anything. But it was affirmation enough that it was already a problem.

"When did you last see Angel?"

She looked at him in surprise. "Not since she handed Sari over."

He stared at her. "Seriously?"

"Yes," she said. "That's why I don't understand why she wants anything to do with her now. Sari won't know her."

"What changed in Angel's life that she suddenly cares?" he murmured.

"I don't know. And because of my number one fear, I don't want her anywhere close to me or Sari."

"Did you have to pay a certain amount of money to get Sari?"

"We covered all the legal costs," she said, "but we didn't give her a lump sum. That would feel like paying for or buying my daughter. Angel wanted money for a flight to Vegas, and we paid that. We were happy to get rid of her, if I'm being honest."

"So she just wanted to drop off her daughter and leave?"

"I think so," she said. "We didn't really get into the discussion. She made the offer, and I jumped at it. Then we moved on."

"Now Angel's wanting something different?" He watched as Daniela slowly nodded.

"The trouble is," she confessed, "I don't want to change the conditions. I don't want this situation to change at all. I just want her to stay away from Sari."

"Is that because you're afraid to lose Sari physically, or because you're afraid Sari will form a bond with her biological mother that may be stronger than her bond with you?" When she sucked in her breath, he knew he'd hit a bull's-eye. He reached out and squeezed her hand again. "It's obvious Sari really loves you."

"I know that," she said. "I didn't think I was such a small person that I would be afraid of sharing that love. But I think at the moment that's an issue for me."

When they reached the park, Sari headed toward the large sandbox. Shambhala stayed at her side, tugging at her leash to make sure they were keeping up. She would correct her behavior when he gave the motion, but her choice was always to stay close to Sari.

He gave her enough lead to see how she would react.

Sari got ahead of them, and Shambhala tried to catch up. But she never needed to be in front. She wasn't trying to be alpha; she was just keeping an eye on the little girl.

As they got to the sandbox, Sari made her way to the center, tripped, and landed on her back in the middle of a soft sand pile. She looked up at her mother, her face scrunched up as if she would cry, but then Shambhala bumped her gently with her head on her shoulder. Immediately the storm clouds cleared, and sunshine came through as Sari reached up and threw her arms around Shambhala's head.

Daniela murmured, "It's incredible just how good Shambhala is with her."

"I know," he said. "It's pretty intriguing."

When Sari was settled and busily digging in the sand, Weston brought Shambhala closer to him. Turning to look at Daniela, he said, "I'll just walk around the park a little with the dog. I want to go over some commands to see how she does."

Daniela nodded, and he headed a little distance away from them.

Shambhala let him know she was disturbed at leaving

the little girl. She kept turning to look behind them to make sure Sari was okay.

"It's okay, Shambhala. She's fine."

Shambhala gave him a hard look, and he had to acknowledge an awful lot of guard dog remained in her. Setting to work, he ascertained she remembered her basic training. Then he worked on several others he had looked up after finding out he was coming after a War Dog. A few more he needed to work on to see if she would listen as well. He needed her off-leash and in a fenced area for that. She had all the regular commands down pat, and he was really proud of her for that.

When they walked back with her heeling properly and at his side, her ears picked up and more energy was in her step as they headed to the sandbox, where Daniela and Sari were waiting for them. He smiled, reached down and scratched Shambhala between the ears.

"You really do love that little girl, don't you?" Her tail wagged faster and faster the closer they got, and, as soon as they made it to the sandbox, she hopped in and nudged the little girl.

"Doggy, doggy," Sari cried out and wrapped her arms around the dog.

"You know something?" he said to Daniela. "We may have a harder time separating them than we're thinking."

"I can tell," she said. "I was just thinking that when you came back toward us. The dog was obviously happy to be coming this way."

He nodded. "Let's head home."

She smiled. "That sounds great. But how will you get Sari to do that?"

"Easy," he said. "Sari, come on. Time to go back to the

house."

She looked up at him and shook her head. "No."

He looked at her, surprised, then looked at her mother, who stood there with her arms crossed over her chest and a big grin on her face. "I guess you don't have to, but Shambhala and I are going home." He called Shambhala to his side. Reluctant but obedient, she complied. Then he turned back to look at Sari. "We're leaving now and going back to the house."

As he and Shambhala turned and walked away, Sari started crying and screaming.

He stopped and looked back at her. "So does that mean you're ready to listen and to come home with us?"

She nodded and reached up her hands. Daniela picked Sari up and caught up with Weston and Shambhala.

Weston turned to the little girl. "I'm so glad you came with us. Do you want to ride on my shoulders?"

Immediately the clouds disappeared, and the sun shone once more.

As soon as Daniela put her up on his shoulders, he reached up with one hand and said, "Now, you've got to grab hold of my ears, and I'll hold on to your feet." Her legs were just long enough that he could grab both of her feet with one hand. He looked at Daniela. "Does she have any experience being carried like this?"

She shook her head and, with one hand, gently pushed on the little girl's back to show her how to sit up straight. "I'll just walk back here," she said with a laugh. "The last thing we need is to have her fall backward."

Slowly the procession made its way back to the house.

THE NEXT MORNING, Weston woke up and went downstairs quietly, not wanting to wake either Daniela or Sari. As he walked past her room, he could hear Sari gurgling. He stopped with a smile on his face as he listened to the sounds of a baby waking up. It was something he had never heard before, and it was special. Very special.

He noted that Shambhala lay on the floor by the child's bed.

Soon, he slipped down the stairs as quietly as he could, not sure what Daniela's morning routine was, Shambhala following him. Once in the kitchen, he watched as Shambhala headed to her empty food bowl. He filled it for her and then set about making coffee. When it was ready, he watched as Shambhala returned to Sari's room, while Weston stepped outside onto the patio, where he enjoyed his first cup, watching the sunrise.

He wondered if Daniela was intent on staying up here in Alaska. And then another thought came. If he wanted to keep up a relationship with his daughter, was he prepared to move here? There were things he would have to sort out.

He was amazed at the bond between Shambhala and Sari. Though there was a little tug at his heart when he first met Sari, there hadn't been that immediate, overwhelming connection of "This is my child. I need to be there for her." A part of him wondered if something was wrong with him because that hadn't happened.

He sat here contemplating fatherhood, wondering if someone adapted to having it suddenly sprung upon them. He knew a lot of guys who were baby crazy. It was funny to see, and, while he'd seen many more women who were that way, seeing it in the occasional male was compelling. He hadn't ever had anything to do with babies and didn't feel any need to turn into a simpering idiot because a baby showed up.

At the same time, she was his daughter, and something was between them. It was up to him to foster it, so a bond could form between them. Maybe it was seeing the bond between Shambhala and Sari happen so fast that made him expect something like that for himself. But obviously he needed a fur coat in order to fit the bill. He snickered at his own joke.

"Well, it's nice to see you're having a good morning," Daniela said, but her voice was cross. "Do you think you could give me a hand for a second?"

He bounded to his feet and turned to face her. She had Sari in her arms, only Sari was cranky and wouldn't sit properly. He reached out his hands, taking Sari from her, putting her on his hip. "What's wrong?"

"I don't know," Daniela said, rubbing her eyes. "I had a crappy night. She woke up just fine, but then, within a few minutes, she got crabby. I need a cup of coffee, and I'll get her some food. She often wakes up superhungry."

"That's a family trait on my side. Sorry," he said apologetically.

She looked at him in surprise.

"I always woke up hungry," he said. "The first thing I did, as soon as I was old enough, was get to the cupboards and into the fridge to get myself something to eat."

"Great," she said. "I'll have to start putting snacks out for Sari, so she'll get them first thing in the morning."

"It's not a bad idea," he said. "It's what my parents did."

She shook her head and poured herself a cup of coffee while he watched. He looked down to see Sari staring up at them. Her eyes were huge and deep. It was as if she had decided to withhold judgment on him, depending on how he behaved over the next little while.

"Good morning, Sari. I heard you talking to yourself this morning." She looked at him, her gaze widening at the sound of his voice, and then her face split into a big smile. "That is a much nicer greeting than the first one I got from you," he said, smiling back at her.

She was astonishing and quite substantial. He didn't know what he'd expected her to weigh, but she was so small, he figured he wouldn't really notice it. But suddenly she was leaning back against his arm because she wasn't quite sure she wanted to get any closer. He could actually feel her weight now. "No wonder women get such strong muscles from packing kids," he murmured.

Just then Daniela stepped back outside, holding her cup of coffee. She looked up at the sun, closed her eyes and took several deep breaths.

"How long have you been in Alaska?"

"About five years," she said. She opened her eyes and turned to look at him. "Why do you ask?"

"I was just wondering if this is where you wanted to be," he explained. "If this is where your family and friends are, or if you were open to moving somewhere else."

"I came here because of Charlie. As it happened, my sister was here already. Our parents live in Maine."

"That's a long way to come," he said.

She nodded. "It is," she said. "I'm sure more employment opportunities are in other places, but I do like it here."

"*Like* as in *a lot?*"

Her lips kicked up at the corners. "*Like*," she repeated. "It's hard to love the winters."

He grinned. "For that reason alone, Maine sounds like a

better deal," he said.

"But then, there's the people," she said with a shudder. "And very high real estate."

"True, but there are plenty of other states. New Mexico, for one. How about Oregon? Anything along the West Coast or in the Southwest. You could do quite well in those areas."

She nodded. "But I'd have to have a reason. I can't just pick up and move for no reason. It's hard to uproot her, and I'd still have to have the money to make it happen, which I don't."

"Quite true," he said in agreement.

"Where do you live?"

"I was in New Mexico," he said, "and that's where the group of guys are that I ended up working with before I came here. I was raised in Colorado, but we all left as soon as I was a teenager. My parents live in Arizona."

"I don't think I want to go that far south," she said. "I don't mind four seasons. I think it's stunning to have fall and spring."

"Agreed," he said, "but I'm in the position of having to find a job too."

She studied him for a long moment.

He dropped his gaze to the backyard, where he'd seen a small garden she had tried and then either gave up on or it just wasn't warm enough yet for the sprouts to come up.

"Are you asking for a specific reason?"

"Of course," he said. "We're both facing an uncertain future and are at odd ends. The question is whether we want to align some of our future, so we can make a parental relationship work."

"Oh," she said, then gave a clipped nod. "Of course that makes sense. I'd never considered moving away."

"But you did consider me moving up here?"

She gave him a half grin. "Yeah. Selfish of me, wasn't it?"

He shrugged. "It's reasonable, I think, to expect or want other people to make a change instead of yourself."

"I hadn't considered that," she said, sitting down on the step with a rather hard *thump*. "I would certainly miss my sister."

"Of course," he said. "I don't know that living in another state is what you want. Or if that would be any easier for you."

"I don't know," she said. "Sometimes I think it's better to stay because the memories are here, and then other times I think I'd be better off to get away from the memories. I just get through that day, and then all I can see is getting through the next day, so I don't really think about down the road to some different future."

"Understood," he said with a smile.

As soon as she finished her coffee, she stood. "Let's bring her inside, so we can get breakfast."

He took Sari in, set her in her high chair, and she grinned up at him. He pulled up a chair beside her and sat down. "What does she normally have for breakfast?"

"Her favorite is toast." It wasn't long before the toaster popped up.

Sari picked up a piece and started munching away.

Weston laughed. "Does she get most of it in her mouth?"

Daniela's laughter made his smile even brighter. "She does eventually," she said. "But, in the meantime, there'll be butter everywhere, particularly in her hair."

And just as she said that, he watched Sari run her mucky

fingers over her head. He grinned. "You must spend a lot of time with her in the bath."

"Washcloths do a pretty good job," she said cheerfully. She came back over with another piece of toast cut into little squares.

He looked at it with interest as she put some peanut butter on it and handed over one square. "Only one square?"

"Yes," she answered. "Sari likes to lick off the peanut butter but doesn't eat most of the bread." She looked over at him. "What would you like for breakfast?"

"Normally I eat a fairly big breakfast," he said, "but I don't want to put you out or eat you out of house and home. I can always go to town and pick up something or go to a restaurant."

She waved her hand at him. "Nonsense. You do remember you gave me a pile of cash yesterday, right? But you'll need to tell me what you mean, when you say, *a big breakfast.*"

"Bacon and eggs or something like that for a start," he said. "I can cook it if you have the ingredients."

She looked at him, surprising him with a nod. "I think we can manage that." She walked to the fridge, pulled out a pack of bacon and a dozen eggs. "Anything else?"

He looked in to see a couple cold baked potatoes on the rack and spoke up. "Were you saving those potatoes for anything?"

She shook her head. "Nope. If you want them, go for it."

He snagged them both and chopped them into little pieces, frying them in a pan with the bacon. When everything was done, he moved it all off to the side, cracking a couple eggs and adding them to the pan. When he had the eggs cooked the way he liked, he used the spatula to put it all onto a plate, took it to the table and sat down beside them. He noticed that Daniela had just toast too, along with her daughter.

He stopped, looked at her plate and asked, "You can have half of this, if you'd like."

She chuckled. "Then it wouldn't be a big breakfast, would it?" she teased.

"I should have asked if you wanted some. I'm embarrassed I didn't."

"I don't eat breakfast," she said. "I don't have much appetite in the morning."

"Good to know," he said.

With that, he dug into his breakfast. Sari watched him with fascination. He looked at her as she started banging her high chair tray. "Would she eat any of this?"

"It's all good food for her," she said, "so you can try her with some of it."

He picked up a piece of bacon, snapped off a little bit and handed it to her. She grabbed it from his hand and put it in her mouth. Almost a blissful look came over her face. He laughed. "Maybe I shouldn't have done that."

"No, maybe not," Daniela said with a heavy sigh. "She does like your food, so that's a good thing. But trying to keep some foods in the house is not an easy job."

"Not at all," he said. "But you're doing a lovely job with her."

She looked at him in surprise. "You mean, all that you've seen in the last day or two."

He shrugged. "Well, so far, it's all I've got," he said. "The house is clean. Sari looks great. She's eating well, and she's happy. You care deeply about her, and she adores you, so it's obvious she's doing very well in your care."

She noticeably relaxed at that, which made him realize just how much fear was inside her.

"Did you really expect me to try to take her away from you?"

She gave him a flat glare. "*Expect*, no, but people are people. So while I certainly didn't want to entertain the idea, it's hard not to be concerned."

"I understand," he said.

Just then her phone rang. She looked at it and gasped.

"What's wrong?"

"It's Angel," she said.

"You might as well answer it," he said. "We need to deal with this one way or another."

She looked at him with fear evident in her eyes.

"Put it on Speakerphone."

She did as he asked and set the phone on the table, taking a deep breath. "Angel, what's up?"

"I want to come see my daughter," Angel said abruptly.

"Why is that?" Daniela asked.

There was silence at first. "She is my daughter," Angel said belligerently.

Weston was interested in her tone of voice. Nothing in there said Angel missed her daughter and wanted to see her or that Angel was heartbroken at having given her up. Angel spoke as if Sari were a possession—as if she had ownership. He just nodded at Daniela to keep the conversation going.

"She's not your daughter anymore, Angel," Daniela said calmly. "I have the paperwork to prove it."

"You can't keep her from me," Angel said.

"I don't know about that," Daniela replied. "The thing is, this is the first time in eighteen months you've even bothered to contact me about her. So why now?"

"Well, maybe I just want to see her now," Angel said.

"I don't think so," Daniela murmured.

"What? Do you think you're the only mother around?" Angel snapped. "You're not a real mother anyway," she said. "I'm the mother. You're just a babysitter. This isn't over, and, when you least expect me, I'll be there."

At that, Western snatched the phone and said, "That's a very interesting comment you just made there, Angel."

Suspicious, she said, "Who's there? Who is that?"

"Sari's father," Weston said in a silky voice, as he looked over at Daniela. "I'm here for a visit with my daughter."

A shocked silence came on the other end of the phone. "God, why would she want you there?" Angel said, her voice snide as always. "And just because you're there doesn't mean I can't be. That's my daughter, and you're not keeping her from me."

"Like Daniela said, it's interesting that you haven't wanted anything to do with Sari all this time. Why now, Angel? Did you find a buyer for her? Is there something you want? Drug money, perhaps? Did you end up in a slum somewhere and need cash to pick up your game?"

Angel laughed. "You don't know anything about me. But you will. You will." And, with that, she hung up, leaving the two of them staring at each other across the phone.

CHAPTER 10

"DID SHE JUST threaten you?"

"Both of us and definitely Sari," Weston said, turning his head to study the little girl, who happily chewed away on her toast. "And she hasn't contacted you at all in this last year and a half?"

"Not once," Daniela said, bewildered. "What did you mean about her being out of money or finding a buyer? You're not implying she would steal Sari and sell her to somebody. Are you?"

"Do you consider that she sold her to you?" he asked, turning her words around.

She glared at him for a long moment. "*Sell*, no. Gave, yes. And, yes, I paid for all the legal work, but, like I told you, I didn't give her any money for Sari."

"Did you give her any money so she could leave?"

"Not cash," she said in surprise. "But, as I told you already, when she wanted a flight out of here, I paid for a ticket."

"I would have too," he said. "Anything to get her away from here."

"Exactly," she said. "Sari was skinny and crying all the time, when we first got her, so I'm not even sure how much Angel was feeding her. I'm pretty sure she didn't nurse her at all."

"How old was she?"

"According to her birth certificate, she was about one month old."

"So you took her and then started the paperwork?"

"Yes, that's exactly what happened."

He nodded but said nothing.

"Is she serious?"

"We'll assume so," he said calmly. "And hope she isn't. I'll call in some favors and do some research to see if we can figure out what Angel's been up to for the last year and a half."

"What will that tell us?"

"It should tell us if she's gotten into a bad crowd or has financial difficulties—like owing loan sharks—what kind of drugs she may be into, or if she's just looking for enough money for another ticket somewhere."

"Which I would gladly pay," Daniela said immediately.

He smiled gently. "I know you would because you want the problem to go away. Angel knows that too. But what happens when a plane ticket isn't enough to make her go away?"

She blanched. "You're talking blackmail?"

"I'm not sure what I'm saying here, but I'm sure you can see how that could happen. Angel knows you're petrified she'll try to get Sari back, and you'll do anything to stop that from happening."

"But I don't have any money," she said faintly.

"Anybody you can borrow from?"

She nodded. "Sure. But I don't know when I'd ever be able to pay them back."

"Angel won't care about that," he said. "If that's what she's after, and, as long as she gets it, she won't care where it comes from."

"I didn't think this would happen," she said, springing to her feet. Soon she was pacing the kitchen. Sari picked up on her distress and started to cry. Daniela rushed to her, lifted the little girl out of the high chair, took her to the sink, where she wiped down her hair, face and hands. "It's all right, sweetie. Mommy's fine. I'm sorry. I didn't mean to upset you."

The little girl wanted to be convinced, so it didn't take too long for the sunshine to return to her face.

Daniela put her down on the floor.

Sari headed right for Shambhala, who was lying in front of the glass doors. She sat down with a hard *thump*, giving the dog a hug. Shambhala lay back down again, only now with a little girl curled up beside her.

Daniela looked back at Weston. "What do we have to do?"

"I need to see the paperwork you have for the adoption, so we can see if it's locked down or if there is anything Angel can use to get contact or to attempt to reverse the adoption."

"And if she does? Then what?" she cried out. "I can't live without Sari, Weston. I've spent my whole life getting to this point, and I've looked after her all this time. She's my little girl."

"Easy," he said. "I get where you're coming from, but let's find out just how much damage Angel could legally do."

"And you're her father," she said, hating to hear the weakness in her voice. "Is that what you're trying to do? To see if you can try to take Sari too?"

He looked at her with surprise. "Why would I do that? It's obvious you're taking perfect care of her. Look at her."

"But she's your daughter," she said in confusion. "She's

all I ever wanted."

"I get that," he said. "But I never thought I would have that. So now that I do, I'm still working my way around to what's right. It's a complicated issue."

She shook her head sadly. "It's not complicated," she said. "You are her father. You want to have her in your life, or you don't." And, on that note, she spun on her heels and left the kitchen.

Is it that simple, he wondered. He pulled out his phone and contacted Badger. "I have an odd wrinkle," he said when Badger answered.

"What kind of a wrinkle?"

"The biological mother of my child has turned up, making threats. Can you help me figure out some things?" Then he explained the scenario and what had just happened.

"When you get a copy of the paperwork, send it to me," Badger said. "We'll take a look at where things stand legally. It's quite possible it wasn't a legal deal. You know that, right?"

"I know," he said. "The thing is, Sari has a great mom and a stable life with Daniela. The biological mother is a train wreck just waiting to happen."

"Families have been torn apart over less," Badger said. "Plus I don't think courts look kindly upon drunk mothers with many different sex partners. Regardless, she's your daughter, so you have rights too." He stopped for a moment. "Do you know for sure she's your daughter?"

"No," Weston said. "I don't know that for sure. I certainly wondered, but I could see the family resemblance as soon as I saw her. I guess it's something I should confirm though."

"Send us DNA. We can rush it to a private lab and get results back pretty fast," Badger said. "I think that'll be one of the first things. Because, if Angel does have a leg to stand on, so do you, and it might require that leverage in order to find a good solution to this." Badger stopped for another long moment. "How do you feel about being a father now?"

"She's adorable," Weston said warmly. "And I'm slowly coming around to the fact that she really exists. As for the future, I have no clue. But I think I would like to watch her grow up."

"*Think?*"

"Hey, that's progress. Yesterday I wasn't even sure about that," he said. "What I can tell you is, Shambhala has completely adopted her, and Sari's adopted the dog. I'll send you some photos."

"Good enough," he said. "We will check into the law in Alaska. Talk to you soon."

Just then, Daniela walked back into the kitchen with an envelope and held it out. "The adoption papers."

He nodded and reached for the envelope. As far as he could see, everything looked okay. "Do you have a scanner?"

She shook her head.

He nodded his understanding. "I can take pictures." He took photos of everything in the envelope and sent them all off to Badger. When he was done, he turned to her. "I have another difficult request, and I don't want you to take it wrong."

Her face shut down. "What is it?"

"I want to take DNA swabs from Sari's mouth and mine, to test to make sure she's my daughter."

Anger flashed in her gaze.

He shook his head. "Not to prove that she isn't," he said gently, "but to prove that she is, in case we end up with court issues. A father does have rights, and no judge will allow me to have any input if I can't prove it. Angel could just as easily stand up in court and say she slept with six other guys, and I'm not the father."

Daniela stared at him in surprise and then nodded. "I don't know why I didn't think of that," she said. "Angel told me that you were the father, and I just believed it blindly."

"Turns out, you can't believe a whole lot about what Angel says," he said.

Daniela looked at her daughter. "So what do we have to do?"

"It's simple actually," he said. "But we should do it as soon as possible."

"Just tell me what to do," she said with a nod.

CHAPTER 11

DANIELA HADN'T EVER thought to check that he was the father, but, when they got back from overnighting the mouth swabs and hair samples to Badger, she clearly wondered. "You said you were only with Angel for one night?"

"Yes," he said.

"So it's quite possible you aren't the father."

"It's a possibility, yes." And that possibility tormented him. Already a bond was growing where he wanted Sari to be his, and what if they found out she wasn't?

"I don't know why I just believed her," she cried out. "This could change everything."

"Which is also why we have to find out," he said calmly. "Information is everything."

She stared at him. "Sure, but it could also be the end of my world."

"No," he said, giving her a light shake. "You adopted Sari. Me being the father or not doesn't impact that. Angel hasn't had anything to do with you and your daughter all this time, and now suddenly she comes back around? A judge will not just turn around and give her back."

Taking a deep, slow breath, Daniela said, "I want to believe you."

"Good," he said.

"But it's damn hard."

"Of course it is," he said. "As far as you're concerned, Sari is yours. And you'll do everything in your power to defend her."

She looked up at him and nodded. "It's a good thing you understand that, Weston, because it's the truth. And that goes for you too."

He shook his head. "I am not trying to take her away from you. Look at me, Daniela. I wouldn't do that to Sari. And I wouldn't do it to you."

She took another slow, deep breath and then finally began to relax. "Thank you," she said. "I really needed to hear that."

"I'm sorry you're still so insecure about her," he admitted. "And I can understand why." He motioned at the phone. "Angel's not helping."

Daniela snorted. "Angel is a menace. It was fine when she was out of our lives, but, now that she's come back, it feels very much like a threat."

"I agree," he said. "But we can deal with this."

She nodded and didn't say anything more. As much as she wanted to continue the discussion, she also wanted to get away from it. She hopped up and said, "Are you up for a cup of coffee?"

"Always," he said distractedly. The idea that Sari might not be his had thrown him for a loop.

She put on a pot of coffee, turned around and asked, "What will you do about Shambhala?"

He shrugged. "No decision as of yet. We need to sort out this Grant situation first."

She nodded. "That's just too bizarre."

"Insane," he said with a heavy sigh. "I'll do some research. Do you mind if I work at the dining room table?" He looked at her as he started toward his room. He stopped, waiting for her to give him an answer.

She smiled. "Sure, no problem."

She watched him go up the stairs. He was a huge man and very controlled. Obviously Angel's call had bothered him too, and that was good. Because this was still his child. At least she hoped it was. God, what if he wasn't Sari's father? What if someone else was the father? Someone more like Angel? She turned, looking at her daughter, just shaking her head. "You can't do anything about it, so let it go," she murmured to herself.

When the coffee was done dripping, she poured two cups and took one to the dining room table. She left it there and then headed back, coaxing Sari into the playroom, where she could play some more with her building blocks. There Sari was happy for at least half an hour, with Shambhala just lying on the floor nearby, watching her. Finally Sari stopped, looked at Daniela and said, "Play outside?"

Daniela looked outside, then nodded. "Why not?" she said with a smile. "We could probably use some fresh air." She hopped up to her feet, scooped up Sari and took her daughter to the closet, where she dressed Sari in a light jacket and boots. Hopefully she wouldn't be too hot. A bit of rain came through the night, so Daniela wasn't sure if anything was wet but decided it didn't matter anyway.

Sari headed to the swing set on her own. With her coffee in hand, Daniela walked over and set the cup on the ground, while she helped Sari get in the baby seat, and then gently swung her back and forth.

Shambhala had followed them outside and lay on the grass. Daniela worried about keeping the dog, as she hadn't had much experience with dogs herself. And she worried about not keeping the dog, as attached as the dog and her daughter had become.

Shambhala seemed to be devoted to Sari and hadn't shown any sign of aggression, but it was hard to know how much was influenced by Weston's presence, since he was an experienced handler. Or maybe there hadn't yet been the right situation where things could end up ugly.

Of course she didn't want that to happen. Enough had been ugly in her world that she didn't want any more. When she turned around to check on Weston, he still sat at the dining room table on the phone, his fingers clicking away on the laptop even as he spoke to someone.

She wasn't even sure what he did for a living. Though she wasn't sure he knew either, since he had said something about finding a job. That brought her back around to how she would feel if she left Alaska. It wasn't the easiest of states to live in, especially since the winters were harsh and long. She had grown accustomed to it. But was it more of a safety net because it was comfortable? Winters would certainly be a lot easier if she moved anywhere farther south, and it wasn't like she was limited to California. Even if she went to Colorado and stayed away from the mountain ski areas, it wouldn't be too bad for her and Sari.

She didn't know what to do.

As she gently pushed Sari back and forth, her phone rang. She pulled it from her pocket to see her sister was calling. "Hey," she said. "What's up?"

"I don't know," Davida said. "I just keep getting a weird feeling about you. Are you okay?"

"I'm fine," Daniela said with a laugh. "You and your feelings."

"Hey, you know you learn to trust certain things," her sister said.

"I hear you. Anyway, we're all good here."

"And what about him?" her sister asked.

"He's doing fine too," she said in a neutral tone, not wanting to go down that path.

"I would invite you and Sari over for a meal this weekend, but I'm not sure I want to invite him too. When is he leaving?"

"Not sure yet," Daniela said cheerfully, quite happy to have a reason to sidestep the dinner, which was sure to be an inquisition. "Don't worry about it. We'll do dinner after he's gone."

"Perfect," her sister said with a sigh of relief. "But when is that?"

"Don't know. I'll keep you posted." And, with that, she hung up. She had no doubt that her sister's invitation for a meal was heartfelt but knew she was fishing for information. And Daniela really wasn't up for that.

"Are you okay?"

She smiled over at Weston. "Just my sister."

"I gather she's not happy I'm here?"

She shrugged. "Doesn't matter if she is or not," she said lightly. "This is what I chose to do."

He smiled at her. A warm and caring smile that made her heart go soft. Dangerous signs, but, like a moth to a flame, she felt helpless to do anything but react to this man. She didn't know why she felt it was so necessary to bring him into Sari's life. But she had, and now that he was here, she wanted him in her life as well.

"I'm going out for a few hours," he said.

"Now?" she asked in confusion.

He caught her glance, nodded and said, "It's connected to Grant."

"Can I go with you?"

He stopped, looked at her in surprise and then shook his head. "No, I'll go talk to some people who knew Grant and his brother. I'm trying to figure out if either had any mannerisms that would help us identify who's who."

She looked at Sari and realized it was probably better that her daughter didn't go. "Okay," she said. "Will you be here for dinner?"

"Steaks, remember?"

She chuckled. "Only if you buy them," she said. "That's out of my price range, even with the money you gave me."

"No problem," he promised.

She watched as he headed to his rental truck. Sari came to her side as Shambhala walked next to Weston, then hopped into the truck with him. Daniela realized he must have given a command to the dog that she hadn't noticed.

"Doggy," Sari cried out, her hand pointed in the direction of Shambhala.

"Don't worry. Doggy and Daddy will come home later," Daniela said absentmindedly. At that, Sari went silent. Daniela looked down at her and realized what she had said. "Yes, baby, that's your daddy." She wasn't sure if she should have said anything in case the DNA came back the wrong way, but still it seemed wrong not to say something. Sari looked up at her, then looked back at the truck as it disappeared down the road. She didn't say anything for a time, and it was obvious she was processing. "It's okay, sweetheart. They'll be back."

She looked down at Sari, who still stared out at the now-empty road. Turning her face back to Daniela, her bottom lip trembled. "It's all right. They'll come home," she said again. She reached her arms down as Sari reached up, wanting a hug. She picked up the little girl and walked back inside. For better or for worse, right now they were alone again. If Weston didn't stay, she would have to get used to that. Which was okay; she'd been alone a lot for the last few years. She could do this.

She needed to focus on what she would do when he left. And that meant finding a better job and potentially day care. And hopefully wages that would allow that to work. Online or work from home would be the best.

On that note, she put on the teakettle and headed to her laptop with Sari at her side. "Don't you worry, little one. Mommy's got this."

WESTON HEADED INTO town, wondering what he was supposed to do, but knowing that staying there in a comfy cozy family setting was both a draw he couldn't really afford to let distract him and yet something he didn't want to resist. He had brought up a *parental* relationship earlier in his discussion with Daniela, but his mind was already going further into the relationship area. It made no sense, but he didn't know if it was his daughter—which was the sweetest sounding word he'd ever heard—or if it was Daniela herself. She was one seriously attractive woman, both outside and inside.

No doubt he could succumb to that whole sweet family setting, but she wasn't his wife, and, although he felt Sari was his daughter, legally she wasn't. It was a screwed-up deal, and it was playing with his head. He really liked what he saw and loved how he felt, but that didn't make any of it a reality.

As he drove into town, his first stop was a grocery store, where he picked up steaks. With the temperature in Anchorage in July well above freezing, he also picked up a small cooler and some ice, because it'd be hours before he returned home. Shambhala was more than interested in the package. When he returned to the truck, he put the meat and the ice into the cooler, and placed it and a few other necessities behind the seat, safely out of the dog's way.

Hopping back into the truck, he and Shambhala headed to the police station. When he walked in, he asked if he could see the detective. He'd sent a message earlier but hadn't received a response. The front desk contacted the detective, and, sure enough, while Weston stood here waiting in the small front office, Detective Kruger came through an inner door. He motioned for Weston to follow him.

As they headed in to his office, he offered a seat. "Can I get you a coffee?"

"Sure," Weston said with a smile. He had Shambhala at his side, and she lay down at his feet. She seemed completely unconcerned being in the office with him. And the detective hadn't had a problem either apparently.

When the detective came back though, he noticed the dog for the first time. "I forgot she went home with you," he said. "I still think of her as Grant's."

"But you took Grant away, and I couldn't leave the dog there."

"Agreed," the detective said. "Grant has been released, by the way."

That was news to Weston. "Interesting. No reason to hold him?"

"Not yet," he said. "His story is beyond odd, but, even though he's a twin, his DNA will still be unique."

"I wondered if anybody would know Grant or the brother enough to identify which one may have died."

"I'm not sure," the detective said with a frown. "It's possible, but I don't have much of a list." He pulled the file toward him and opened it. "Ginger had more friends than Grant did."

"Before they went homesteading, did either of them work in town?"

"Grant used to work at the feedstore, actually."

"You'd think he would have stayed part-time while he was homesteading," Weston said. "It's not like a whole lot of money is in homesteading."

"No, but Grant wasn't exactly one of the hardest-working people I know either. Still, he did do a lot of work on the house, and he had taken a job up north to bring in more money, so he was stepping up." He thought about the dog then. "After the accident, I'm not surprised Shambhala went to the feedstore, since she would have known some of the guys there."

"You're right. The dog is fairly identifiable with a missing leg, not to mention the eye."

"Exactly."

Weston frowned. "Mind if I go back to the feedstore and talk to them?"

"Feel free," the detective said. "But, as far as we're concerned, we don't really have any reason to exhume the other body, and we don't have any reason to suspect that this person is anyone other than Grant."

"Maybe, but then you have a body buried under the wrong name."

The detective shrugged. "Grant does want the name on the stone changed."

Weston sat back and thought about that. "That's just way too convenient for my taste," he announced.

"Mine too," the detective agreed. "But budgetary constraints come into play here."

"What about Ginger's family?"

"As far as I know, she's a local gal. Her parents passed away a few years back. I don't think she has any siblings."

"What about children?"

"I think she does have one or two. From a previous marriage. I've spoken to her ex-husband, and he's told his family. Why?"

"Just wondering if they were old enough to be a factor here. If we do know for sure Gregory died in the accident," he said, "you're not exhuming and looking for a cause of death?"

"An autopsy wasn't done at the time because the crash was a fairly obvious cause of death," the detective said. "I doubt the kids are involved. They don't have anything to do with their mother and aren't in the will."

"Sure, but now it seems you're closer to having a motive for murder."

"Maybe, but we don't have anything other than a possibility," the detective said. "Mark my words. If we do have reason to believe, that's different, but, at the moment, we don't."

"Good enough." Weston hopped to his feet, intent on leaving.

Then the detective asked, "Did you really come here for the dog?"

"I came here because of both the dog and my daughter,"

Weston said. "Speaking of which, how do things work in terms of an adoption up here?" He explained the situation and what had happened with Angel.

"If Daniela has proper papers," the detective said, "then the child is hers. But if something was shady about the process and the paperwork used, then who knows what a judge might entertain."

"Meaning, if the adoption skirted the legalities, it could be ruled null and void, and the biological mother could get the child back. Correct?"

"Let's just say that the biological mother would have a lot more power and a better chance of getting her daughter back. Particularly if she comes up with any proof she was pressured into giving away her child."

"And considering that I'm the father, do I have any rights?"

"Just as much as the mother apparently," the detective said. "But, even if she was pressured into doing it, she hasn't shown up for all this time. But then, neither did you." There was no pulling a punch on that one.

Weston nodded. "I didn't even know about her," he said. "I found out when Angel called me drunk one night, but, by then, the adoption was already done. I had no idea what to do. Daniela contacted me not long ago."

"And this Angel seems pretty positive you're the father?"

"That's what she said to me and to Daniela. But what she would say to a judge is anybody's guess. We're actually waiting on DNA."

"That would be good. It would give you more legal cause for a judge to grant you custody."

"What if I'm content to have Daniela keep her?"

"It's hard to say. If the judge doesn't want that, it will

become between you and Angel."

"In that case, I'd fight to get her myself," he said firmly. "Angel's not a fit parent."

"Then you should probably prepare for a legal defense, just in case."

"And, if Angel does want Sari, for some nefarious reason, … like blackmail," he said, letting his voice trail off.

"If that's the case, you let me know," he said. "Because that is something I can act on. If she gets into criminal behavior we can prove, then she can be charged."

"Right," Weston said, "but, in the meantime, it could get ugly."

"Yes," the detective said. "These things are just sad. And, if she didn't want the child in all that time, you have to wonder why she wants her now."

"That's exactly the problem. I don't get a good feeling about any of this."

"Doesn't matter if you do or not. Stay on the good side of the law, and hopefully the paperwork is in order, and it won't be an issue."

"Right, well, we're working on that," Weston said. "I've got the paperwork in to a lawyer, so we know where we stand there."

"I can take a look, if you want to send it to me."

Figuring it couldn't hurt, Weston brought it up on his phone and emailed the documents. The detective printed it off, sat back to look at it. "I can get somebody in the department here to take a look at this. It looks aboveboard to me, but I'm not a lawyer."

"Neither am I, which is why I was looking for a second opinion."

"So Daniela had a lawyer when this was originally drawn

up?"

"Yes," Weston said. He searched his email and frowned. "I don't have the name of the lawyer here, though I can text her for it."

He sent Daniela a text, and, while he and the detective discussed the paperwork, they waited for a response. When it came in, he shared the name with the detective, who nodded.

"That is a reputable firm, so things are looking better and better in that regard."

Weston felt a wave of relief at that news. "That is great to hear. At the time of the adoption, Daniela was married, and her husband has since passed away."

"That's always a problem too," the detective said. "This is a generality, of course, but, when there are issues, and custody cases come before a judge, the stability of the homes is a consideration—like, if there is a dispute, and any chance of a decision being reviewed, if one party is married and is in a more stable situation, often that can influence the decision of the judge."

"Meaning, the judge would prefer to have Sari raised by a husband and wife?"

"Yes."

As Weston left the police station, he wondered about contacting the lawyer's office himself. He hopped into his vehicle, wondering if the office could still be open, and brought the firm up on his GPS. When he realized it was just around the corner and a couple blocks away, he drove over and parked in a back lot up the street.

Shambhala strode happily along at his side, seemingly content to just be with somebody and to have a purpose. Weston reached out a hand and gently scratched her behind the ears as they walked the block. The legal firm was located at the front right corner. He turned the knob, but it was locked. He knocked on the door.

There was no answer, and it was dark inside. He frowned and walked to the adjacent parking lot. A couple vehicles were there, but he didn't know who they belonged to. He went back to the lawyer's office and tried again, but it was definitely locked. Heading to the nearest window, he couldn't see anything because of the shutters, but, as he walked to the other edge, a little bit of space provided him a look inside. He peered through the window, and his heart froze. He couldn't be sure because of the shades blocking his view, but somebody appeared to be lying on the floor.

Swearing, he called the detective. "Hi, it's Weston. I'm at the lawyer's office. I can't get into the front door. It's locked, but I'm looking through a window I can barely see through, and it looks like somebody's on the floor in there."

"Be right there," the detective said, his voice brisk. "It would be pretty shitty timing if it happened to be the lawyer in this case," he said and hung up.

"It wasn't just shitty timing," Weston thought. "It could be catastrophic." He headed back to the front door and rattled it again. There should be another door. He walked around back and found a second door. It was unlocked. With the dog at his side, he pulled it open, propped it open with a rock and stepped inside. Immediately the smell of death assailed him. Shambhala let out a whining howl. He reached down and comforted her.

"You're right, sweetheart. That's not something either of us wants to smell again, is it?" He debated going in, then realized the detective would have his hide for potentially damaging a crime scene. As it was, he didn't have to wait long because the detective was here in a matter of minutes.

Weston stood at the open door, as the detective drove up into the parking lot. As soon as he saw him, the detective frowned.

"Have you been in there?"

Weston shook his head. "No. As soon as I opened the door—which was already unlocked—we could smell it, and we stopped."

"I hope so," he said, "because I won't be happy if you compromised the scene."

"I didn't," Weston said calmly. "I do know how this works."

"Maybe." The detective went in, took one look around, came back out, already on his phone. He looked over at Weston and said, "It's the lawyer. It's his office, and he's dead."

"Anybody else in there?"

"Not that I saw. I'd like you to stick around, so we can get your statement."

He nodded. "Any chance I can go ahead and take a look?"

The detective just looked at him with a hard glare.

"I do have some experience with this and obviously have a personal interest here," he said with a shrug.

"All the more reason not to," the detective said smoothly.

At that point, Weston realized he really would get shut out. He nodded and stepped back with Shambhala. They waited outside until a young officer came over to talk to him. Weston gave him the little information he had, then drove off, heading straight to the feedstore. It looked like Daniela would need a new lawyer.

CHAPTER 12

I T WOULDN'T BE so bad trying to get some work done, except for the fact that Daniela kept getting phone calls with nobody on the other end. After the third call from Private Caller and yet nobody there, Daniela slammed down her phone beside her in frustration, only to see Sari looking up at her with tears in her eyes. Immediately she felt terrible and raced over to pick up her little girl. She tossed her in the air, playing with her until the sunshine came back into her face.

"It's fine, silly," she said. "I don't know who's trying to get a hold of me though."

"Daddy," she said.

At that Daniela froze. "No," she said. "It's not Weston."

"Doggy," the little girl tried again.

"I don't think the doggy knows how to use the phone yet." She walked into the kitchen to put on the teakettle and realized Weston had been gone for a couple hours already. She sent him a quick text, asking if he would make it home for a six o'clock dinner.

She got a strange answer back.

Yes, if I can make it.

She didn't know what that meant, but, if they weren't having steak, she needed to do something else. But, for her and Sari, dinner didn't have to be a big deal, only if she was expected to feed him too.

When she'd made a cup of tea, she headed back, and, as she sat down, her phone rang again. She picked it up, saw it was a Private Caller, and she clearly and succinctly told the other person to take a hike. Then she hung up. As she slammed down the phone again, she thought she heard a voice. But she checked, and the call had ended. She waited for a call back, but there was nothing. She started thinking there might be a problem, and what she had taken as an interfering prank caller with time on his hands might have been a person in distress. She frowned at that.

It was hard, almost impossible to get back to her work now. And when the phone rang again a few minutes later, she picked it up with relief when she saw it said Private Caller. When she hit Talk, she said hello; again there was nothing. "Are you in trouble?" she asked. "Do you need help?" She strained to hear any answer, but there was nothing. Finally, she put the phone back down and ended the call.

"Stuff it," she said. "I don't know who it is, but they can stop hassling me."

When Weston got home, she'd get him to take a look at it. But she hated to depend on him more than she already was. Just having him here when Angel was causing trouble was huge. But she didn't want it to become a habit, and she didn't want him to think that she couldn't live without him. Because, at some point, he would go home. If she didn't move to a state where he lived, chances were she would remain alone.

The phone rang yet again, and she stared at it with growing frustration. Finally she picked it up. "Hello." This time she heard laughter on the other end. Her stomach sank.

"Is this Angel? What's wrong? Are you high on drugs again? You'll never get your daughter back if you're just a druggie," she demanded. "Leave me alone."

"Oh my, you're getting a little unnerved," Angel said. "What's the matter?"

"As if you don't know," Daniela said in disgust. "You've got nothing better to do than make prank phone calls all day or what?"

"This is the first call I've made today," Angel said.

But her tone was mocking. Daniela didn't know if she should believe her or not, so chose the *not*.

"Not likely," Daniela said. "What brought you back to town anyway? Last I saw you, you were desperate to leave here."

"Maybe I missed the place," Angel said.

"You couldn't wait to get out before," Daniela said. "So I doubt it."

"I never did say, *Sorry about Charlie's death*," Angel said abruptly.

"No need to say it now either then," Daniela answered smoothly.

"He was such a sweetheart," Angel said. "Especially in bed."

Daniela froze. "Well, Angel, if you were one more of his many floozies in the last few months of his life, I hope you enjoyed sleeping with a dying man," she said softly. "I certainly didn't mind him enjoying life for a while." It was a lie of course. She had just wanted him to enjoy life with her, not with a million other women.

"You really don't mind that he was sleeping with women back then?" Angel asked in surprise.

"I've come to terms with it. Let's put it that way," Daniela said. "He was very sick, obviously very sick emotionally and mentally as well. Besides, look at his partners," she said with an attempt at a smear. "Most of them were drug addicts and women who he never would have touched if he was healthy."

Angel reacted like she'd been slapped, and you could almost hear her growling on the other end of the phone. "I'm not a drug addict," she snapped.

"You're not exactly a prime citizen either," Daniela said, smiling as she felt she had the upper hand.

"You just keep threatening me and treating me like this," Angel said. "You'll get your own."

"You're the one doing the threatening," Daniela said. "I haven't said anything."

"Well, you're not treating me nice, and, if you want to be the mother of my child, you need to," Angel said, her voice returning to normal, bringing the conversation back again to a threat.

"No. You're forgetting something, Angel. I already am the mother to Sari." And, on that note, she hung up and set the phone off to the side. She wouldn't answer it again.

WESTON HEADED OUT to the feedstore, not that the dog needed more dog food by any means. But, with a leash on her, he walked around the back of the yard, looking to see just how much anybody would have seen of her.

"Can I help you?"

He turned to see the same young man who'd given him the feed earlier.

"I just wondered who all would have seen this dog in the

last six weeks or so. Outside of you."

"Why?" the kid asked. "I haven't been here the whole time, but not many of the others come out here."

"Ah," Weston said. "I wondered."

"Wondered what?" the boy asked, perplexed. "She's a stray. You came and got her, and she looks like she's taken to you just fine."

"I wanted to know about her old owner," he said. "Did you know Grant Buckman?"

The kid shook his head. "I've not been here very long though," he said, "just over a month now."

"And who used to work back here?"

"Johnny," he said. "Johnny Ryder. But he doesn't work here anymore."

"Why is that?"

"He got fired on account of stealing some cash out of the till. He's done it a couple times, I heard, but this last time he took more than they were prepared to forgive."

"That makes sense," he said, wincing. "What about anybody else who worked in this area?"

The kid placed his hands on his hips. "What do you care?"

"I was looking for somebody who knew Grant," he said.

"You know he's dead, right?"

"I do know that," Weston said. "There appears to be a case of mistaken identity though."

The kid's gaze lit up with interest. He looked back toward the front of the warehouse with a shrug. "I don't think so. I don't think anybody here, I mean, ... Grant used to work here but not for a long time."

"How did you know him?"

"Because of Johnny," he said, "but I didn't really know

Grant. I just know of him."

"Had Johnny worked here long?"

"Years and years," the kid said in disgust. "I hope I'm not here for very long."

"You don't like your job?"

"Who could like a job like this?" the kid said. He gave an irritable shrug. "Anyway, you can talk to Johnny. He's probably down at the pub."

"He's got money for the pub?"

"He got another job," the kid said. "Pays more money than here too." He looked around the back warehouse with all the feed stacked up. "But then, anything would pay better than this." He lifted a hand. "I got to go back to work." He walked back inside.

Armed with the name of the establishment, Weston and Shambhala walked back to his truck, hopped in and headed toward the pub. He didn't know if he'd be allowed to take the dog in or not.

As it turned out, a group of men sat outside in a covered patio area. He didn't know which one was Johnny. Just then he heard one of the men call out.

"Hey, Johnny, you owe me a beer!"

A young man in the corner looked up, shrugged and said, "No job, no money. No money, no beer."

The guy just snorted and said, "You've been telling us that for months."

"Been unemployed for months."

And that was inconsistent with what the kid at the feed-store had just said about Johnny. Weston walked into the little courtyard area and walked up to him.

Johnny looked at the dog and smiled. "Well, lookie here."

Shambhala walked over with her tail wagging, and Johnny reached out a gentle hand.

"Right dog, wrong man," he said, looking up and eyeing Weston. "I heard Grant died, so you must have ended up with his dog."

"Yeah, I did," Weston said with a smile. "I understand you knew Grant?"

"Yeah, I did," he said. "I knew him for quite a few years."

"Just from your feedstore job or were you buddies?"

"We used to have a brew together every once in a while," Johnny said. "Once he got married, things got different though."

"Ah, so you knew him from before the marriage?"

"Yeah, he was a good guy," he said. "It's shitty the way he went out, but I guess it was fast."

"Did he have any mannerisms or anything to really help identify who he was?"

"What do you mean?"

"Oh, you know. Things that only he said or did. Physical things you could see and know it was him from across the way. That sort of thing. Things that, if someone described them, you would know they were talking about Grant."

Johnny stared at him with a frown, then smiled. "He'd motion at the table and say, 'If you're going to sit down, you might as well go grab a brew and make it two,'" he said.

Weston laughed. "Good one. Yeah, I can grab a couple beers." He walked to the open door and ordered two through the doorway. Then he sat back down across from Johnny, with Shambhala at his heels. "So, tell me about Grant."

"Not much to tell. He was your average boring old guy

who liked to have a beer and get away from the wife every once in a while."

"He was a twin though," Weston said.

"Yep, he was. He told me about that. He said his brother was a no-good layabout too," Johnny said.

Just then the beers arrived in large tall glasses with a white head of sparkling foam. Weston lifted his glass and took a sip.

Johnny took a hefty slug and sighed happily as he put the glass down, wiping the foam off his mustache. "That was Grant. Just a nice simple guy, enjoying life."

"How'd he hook up with Ginger?"

"No clue," he said, "because she was a lot of woman for him."

"Have you ever met his brother?"

"No, but he said they were identical though." Johnny laughed. "Wouldn't that be a blast? Living your life with a mirror image of yourself."

"Maybe," Weston said. "Might be confusing as hell too."

"Only if the brother was a dick."

"And I guess that's one of my questions for you. What kind of person was his brother?"

"No clue. Grant did say he was a bit of an asshole and superlazy. He didn't like to work. I thought though, even with that, he'd have come up here to look after things."

"But, if they're so alike, then what Grant said meant Grant was an asshole and superlazy too?"

"No, not quite the same thing," he said. "Grant said his brother was a bit of a loser and always looking for the easy way out, or a way to avoid work, instead of just buckling down and getting something done."

"Did Grant have any tattoos or scars? Any accidents or

injuries that you know about? Any way to help identify him? Obviously, they had his body from the accident, but the accident caused injuries to his body, so I'm just asking out of curiosity." Johnny might have been an interesting character, but that didn't mean he was stupid.

Leaning forward with a sharp gaze, he said, "There's more to these questions than you're telling me."

"Just trying to make sure it was Grant they buried," he said.

And with that, Johnny got it. "You think the brother was the one up here, do you?"

"I'm not sure, but possibly Grant's brother was in the vehicle with Grant's wife."

Johnny let out a long whistle. "Now that would be something his brother would do. Apparently he was always getting in trouble over women."

"And you did say Ginger was a lot of woman for Grant."

"Yeah, she sure was. She appeared to be loyal though," he said with a shrug. "But she was a looker. A tall redhead. Hence the name *Ginger*, I guess," he said with a smirk. "Slim, busty, long legs and a bit of a mouth on her. She liked to push him around a little, you know? Be dominant, but he was okay with that. She must have been good in bed. On the other hand, I think Grant was the kind of guy who didn't care either way. He was hooked up emotionally, and she could pretty well get away with anything, and he'd be fine with it."

"Would he though?"

"What do you mean?"

"What if his brother was having an affair with his wife?"

Johnny's eyebrows shot right up to his hairline. "You know something? I don't think he'd be okay with that. The one bee in his bonnet guaranteed to piss him off was his brother. He didn't talk about him often, but, when he did, it was usually venting and in a rage."

"Interesting."

"Why not just contact the brother and see where he is and what his story is?" Johnny asked, leaning back with his glass of beer in his hand again as he took another sip.

"I plan to. I've got a couple calls in but no answer so far." That was at least the truth. He could make all the calls he wanted, but it didn't look like Gregory would be answering anybody. Weston pulled out another Titanium Corp business card and wrote his cell number on the back side. "Listen, Johnny. If you remember anything, give me a shout."

"Why would I call you and not the cops?"

At that, Weston looked at him with a glimmer of a smile. "Because you would never call the cops."

Johnny burst out laughing. "You got that right." Chuckling, he picked up the business card and slipped it into his pocket.

With that, Weston led Shambhala back to the truck. He wasn't sure what else to do, except maybe take those steaks home and enjoy dinner with Sari and Daniela.

CHAPTER 13

A FTER THE STEAKS were cooked, and they'd finished eating, Daniela pushed away her empty plate with a happy sigh. "That was a really good steak."

"And you did a marvelous job on the potatoes and the salad. Thank you," Weston said sincerely.

She smiled. "I've always loved cooking. But cooking for just me and Sari is not the same as cooking for a man."

He nodded. "I tend to eat alone most of the time."

"What will you do now?" she asked curiously.

"I'm not sure," he said. "Like a lot of the guys in my career situation, we're at a crossroads, trying to figure out what we're supposed to do next."

"You have options though, right?"

"Yes," he said. "Lots of options. I just haven't necessarily pinpointed what I want to do, as in a second career."

"You're really good with Shambhala, so you could always do something with dogs. It might be good for her too."

"I think her working days are over," he said, as he put a hand down to the dog, who was ever hopeful and settled at his feet. "She's a music lover apparently. When we get her settled, we'll have to find out what kind of music she likes."

"She's certainly suffered physically, hasn't she?" She studied the poor dog, looking far more battle-scarred than others she'd seen on TV. "She deserves a few years of good rest."

"That is exactly why the government's been checking into making sure these animals are doing okay."

"That is so great. Do you have any new skills or training you picked up while you were in the navy?"

"Lots of them," he said with half a smile. "But not exactly the kind that can land me a job."

"So you didn't pick up any tradesmen certifications or a university degree or anything like that?"

"Lock Picking 101, for example?" He smiled.

She shrugged. "As I don't know exactly what you did in the military ..."

"Secret operations. Usually black ops. Learning to jump out of a plane in the middle of the night and not get fired on was always a popular course."

She laughed and then realized he was serious. She leaned forward. "Wow, you're lucky you're not in the same shape as Shambhala."

"Well, I'm not all that much better," he said. "I was injured pretty badly myself, which is how I ended up retired from active service."

She nodded, wishing she could ask more questions but not wanting to get too personal. "Is there money for retraining?"

"There is. Yes," he said cautiously. "But it still needs to be something I want to do."

"Well, there are things that you want to do, and then there are things that you may need to do while you figure it out," she said humorously.

He shrugged. "I had a few things I was thinking about. I've just come from a center where a bunch of guys like me came together and created a security company, but they're also helping a lot of vets reenter the workforce."

"That's awesome," she said. "I really like the idea of people who've been through something themselves being the ones to help someone else get back into life."

"I volunteered for this job with the dog because I was bored," he said. "I was doing a variety of jobs with them but nothing too major, while I figured out what I wanted to do. Not to worry," he said. "I'll figure it out."

She nodded and didn't say anything.

"Are you looking for support?" he asked abruptly.

She stared at him in surprise and then shook her head. "If you mean, child support, no. I adopted Sari, fully aware of what it would take to raise a child."

"Fully aware as somebody who doesn't have a child could be?" he said gently, and she flushed and nodded.

"That sounded kind of arrogant, didn't it? At the time, it hadn't become clear that Charlie's days were numbered, and things hadn't gone south yet. But back to your question. No, I'm not looking to you to support me or Sari."

"But, on the other hand, why shouldn't I help?" he murmured. He studied the little girl, who smiled up at him.

She was still working on her dinner, which, at the moment, appeared to be mashed carrots. She was working the spoon with a great deal of enthusiasm and not a whole lot of efficiency and splattering carrots all over the floor.

"You almost need a water hose for her, don't you?"

Daniela laughed. "Normally I just feed her and don't give her too much time to play with it," she said. "But we were talking, and she was having fun, so it seemed like a good idea to let her just run with it."

"I'm all for that." Then a particular piece of carrot land-ed close by, and he said, "But we're getting into the danger zone now."

Still chuckling, Daniela grabbed a wet paper towel and removed the plate and the fork from Sari's reach. "You, young lady, are obviously full, if you are throwing your food around."

Sari giggled.

Daniela wiped her down, then lifted her from the high chair and let her run free. She ran right over to Shambhala, tripped and fell over the dog, landing on her belly. Shambhala gently nuzzled Sari's face, then lay back down again.

"I still can't believe how well the two of them get along," Daniela exclaimed.

"I know," he said. "It really restores faith in the bond, doesn't it?"

"Is it hard to figure out what you want to do next?" she asked curiously.

He looked at her smile and saw she was sincere. "For some guys, yes. Most of us think our future, whatever it will be after our service, is down the road much later," he said calmly. "So I wasn't prepared for an accident with an injury that sidelined me long before I started planning my next career move." He showed her half a smile.

She nodded slowly. "Any clue what you want to do?"

"Maybe security," he said. "It's something I certainly know."

"Like a security guard?" That seemed so wrong to her because it seemed like he could do so much more.

He just smiled and said, "That's one aspect to it, but I'm pretty good with computers. I was thinking about setting up a cybersecurity company maybe. I'm not sure yet."

She stared at him, surprised. "That's a huge field, isn't it?"

"It is," he said with a nod. "And I could probably find enough work that I'd have to hire some people pretty fast."

"Then you can hire other guys like you," she said with delight.

He chuckled. "Getting a little ahead of myself there," he said.

She smiled. "But there's time, right?"

"There's time," he affirmed.

Just then her phone went off. Without thinking, she reached for it and saw it said Private Caller. She groaned. "Damn it. It's Angel again."

"Again?"

"Yeah. I had at least four or five calls, but no one ever answered. I finally got frustrated and said something rude. But then I thought I heard someone call out, so I felt terrible and worried someone needed help. And then the next time, it was Angel. But now this one, I don't know." She hit Talk. "Angel, is that you again?"

"Yes, it is," Angel said piously. "Did you think about what I said earlier?"

At Weston's motion, she put the phone on the table and pushed Speakerphone. "Not a whole lot to think about," she said calmly.

"Sure there was. I just didn't give you my terms yet."

Her eyebrows shot up. "Are you serious? You actually want something in order to let me continue being Sari's mother?"

"It's not like your lawyer will back you up, will he?"

"Why not?" Daniela asked, staring down at the phone, then at Weston. And the grim look on his face had her heart sinking. "What are you talking about, Angel?"

"You should read the news first. Don't worry. I'll be calling you back." And, with that, she hung up.

Daniela stared at Weston. "What did that mean?"

"Your lawyer is dead," he said. "I ran by to have a talk with him about the paperwork," he said slowly. "And I found the body in the office. As far as I know, it was your lawyer."

WESTON HADN'T REALLY expected to break the news to her that way. And he really didn't like the idea that Angel was hassling Daniela and coming back around, looking for something more. And he especially didn't like the idea that Angel was already aware of Daniela's attorney's death.

"We'll have to stop Angel somehow." Daniela stared at her phone and realized she had gripped her fingers together so tightly that her knuckles were turning white.

He grabbed both of her hands with his and gently opened them. "Look. Detective Kruger said the paperwork looked like it was all fine and dandy. Let's not get panicked over something we don't know yet is wrong."

She took several deep breaths.

"I realize I'm not the one who should be saying this," he said, "because obviously you're afraid of losing custody, and your feelings are totally understandable. But you're doing a wonderful job, and we have to trust in the system."

"The system doesn't always work," she said softly.

And he could feel the fear rippling up and down her back. He looked down at the phone. "There was no number?"

She shook her head. "No, it kept coming in as Private Caller."

"I wonder if she's using a burner phone."

"If I knew what that was, I might be able to help you," Daniela said, "but I don't."

"Untraceable," he said.

"Why would she do that? And how would she even know to think of it?"

"A very good question," he said, studying her. "Why is she being covert about this at all? That is the bottom line."

"True," she said. "Why doesn't she just show up and ask for five thousand dollars or something?"

He studied her curiously. "Could you do five thousand dollars?"

She looked at him and shook her head. "No, not at all."

He nodded as if that lined up with what he knew. "So, if she knows you don't have any money, why would she be asking you for some?"

"My sister has money," she said sadly. "And she knew my sister too."

"So she'd expect you to go to your sister, but would your sister give it to you?"

Daniela hesitated and then shrugged. "I don't know, and I don't want to find out."

He picked up his phone and sent Badger a text about Angel. **We need more information. She's now making harassing and threatening phone calls. She may have killed Daniela's adoption attorney. Angel's looking for something but isn't being clear as to what she's after.**

"Who are you contacting?" Daniela asked.

"My ex-boss. Or still my boss really, I guess," he said. "We need information on Angel, and we need it now. That's the fastest way to get it."

"If it was so easy to get, wouldn't the detective have it?"

"Sure, but why would he?" he asked.

She looked at him in surprise. "Well, the dead lawyer is Angel's brother."

Stunned, he stopped and stared. "Seriously?"

She nodded. "You didn't know?"

"Of course not." He picked up his phone again and dialed Detective Kruger. When his tired voice answered, Weston said, "So, your case and my case just connected. What I didn't realize is the legal documents I showed you today—the mother, the person who gave over the child—she's apparently the sister of the dead lawyer."

"Interesting," the detective said. "I didn't know that. I suppose we'd have figured it out eventually." There was a moment of silence on the other end. "Oh, and he didn't die today, he was killed yesterday as far as we can tell."

"Wow," Weston said. "Murdered? And he was lying there all this time undetected?"

"Yes," the detective said. "And I hate to ask this, but when did you hit town?"

Weston looked over to see the shock and horror on Daniela's face. "Yesterday," he said. And he gave his flight info. "I've also been with Daniela 90 percent of the time. Or with you."

"Yeah, getting in trouble the rest of time," the detective said with a note of humor.

"Absolutely," Weston said. "But now we need to pursue the Angel line of inquiry."

"I know you were probably a hotshot in the navy," the detective said, "but unless you're actually signing up to do this job that I'm doing on a full-time basis, you'll have to back off and let us do what we do."

"I hear you," Weston said. "But Angel's threatening

Daniela. If you get this solved fast enough, then I'll leave you to it. But if not, well, I do have some resources to bring into play myself." And he hung up.

CHAPTER 14

DANIELA HAD A rough night. She kept waking up. Twice she got up and went to Sari's room to make sure she was still there. Obviously Angel's call had rattled Daniela more than she'd expected. It was pretty distressing to have nightmares like this, but to know a real threat was behind them made it that much worse because it was no longer a nightmare; it was something that was possible.

To lose Sari at this stage would be devastating. Daniela had gone through the process in good faith, believing it was all legal and upfront. But was it? Her husband had handled that aspect of things, and now she had to wonder if she trusted him. While he'd been alive, she had, at least up until his last few months, when she found out he'd been so anxiously spreading love around the world, but now what? Had he done something to deliberately screw her over, like make that paperwork not be legal?

She didn't want to believe he could have been so vindictive. But, toward the end, he had been full of anger, hate and frustration. There definitely hadn't been love.

She tried to push that thought into the back of her mind, as she once again crawled into bed. A branch brushed against her window, making her look out at the early morning darkness. It was still summer here, but winter set in fast and early.

Did she want to leave? She hadn't for all the time she had been here. She'd been totally okay to stay, right up until Weston brought up the possibility of moving south. And now she wondered if she could make that happen somehow. She would miss her sister, but she wouldn't miss the hardship of being here.

Alaskans were a unique breed of people, and she loved them dearly, but she had never really felt like one of them. Five years in Alaska hadn't been enough to make her the same hardy homestead stock most of them were. Of course a lot of the people in the cities were no different here than anywhere else. Would she have an easier time finding a job down South?

She had an online business, so it didn't matter if it moved or not. Could she make it something more full-time so she could afford the higher rents down South, or could she find a place that was a compromise between weather and location, so the rent was still something she could afford? These thoughts only served to keep her emotions flipping from one side to the other as she lay here, dry-eyed, staring as the sun slowly crept up over the horizon. She finally gave up any pretense of trying to sleep and got up, heading into the shower.

As she came out, wrapped in a towel with her robe on, she dressed quickly, feeling a sudden chill in the air. Almost as if a chill were in her soul. Stopping to check in on Sari, she found her daughter sound asleep. Soon she was in the kitchen, and, after she put on the coffee, she stared out at the hills around her home. She was in an odd mood. Everything had suddenly flipped, and she didn't like it. When warm arms wrapped around her, she wasn't even surprised. She leaned into his gentle comfort. "It all feels so weird now."

"I was afraid you weren't sleeping after all of Angel's phone calls."

"And what does the lawyer have to do with any of this?" she exclaimed, twisting in his arms.

He smiled, wrapped her up close and gave her a hug.

Nothing sexual was in it, just comfort. Just somebody who realized she was upset and wanted to help.

And when he stepped back, he walked over to the cupboard and pulled out two coffee cups. As soon as the pot had finished dripping, he poured the coffee. "Shall we enjoy the early morning sun?"

She smiled and took a cup from him and followed his lead outside. "Did you come to any realizations overnight?" she asked.

He looked a little surprised and shook his head. "No," he said. "I've been in this business long enough to know I have to shut down my mind. Otherwise it revolves around and around with no answers. Besides, you need information before you can start making deductions."

She just nodded.

"Or is that not what you meant?" he asked, his gaze on her face.

She smiled and took a deep breath. "This doesn't even feel like home now."

"Why is that?" He frowned.

"I don't know." She had trouble even trying to explain it to herself. "I was fine to stay in Alaska, until you mentioned the possibility of moving elsewhere."

"Ah," he said. "Some suggestions are like that. You don't realize there is another way to live until somebody says, 'Hey, what about this?' Right?"

She nodded. "I have a small budding online business

that can go with me anywhere, as long as I have room for my garden. Plus I was working at the local dollar store, doing temporary shift work, but haven't had a shift in weeks. They keep canceling them."

"And then you have offsetting babysitting costs," he said.

"Yes. Or I have also done babysitting for other people," she said. "And that works well."

"That can't pay too much, does it?"

"It's very irregular and in just short periods at a time," she said.

"So what would you really like to do?" he asked. "If all this trouble with Angel wasn't hanging over your head, would you still be considering a move?"

"I don't know," she said. "A lot about my husband still is here, and a part of me says I need to have a clean break from it all."

"A lot of people find it difficult to leave an area where their spouse or child passed away," he said.

Something searching was in his gaze, and she didn't know quite what it was. She dropped her gaze to look at the yard. "I need to mow this grass," she said nervously.

"I'll take care of it later," he said. "It's too wet at the moment."

She just nodded.

"So tell me about your husband," he said.

Something more than a gentle suggestion was evident in his words. Her back bristled slightly, and then she shrugged. "What is there to say?" she said. "I married him because I loved him, and we were happy for a time, and then we weren't."

Silence. "Well, that's an interesting analysis," he said. "How did he die?"

"I told you. He drove off a cliff."

"Come on. Tell me the rest of it."

"Pancreatic cancer," she said abruptly. "He changed in his last few months. The treatment kept him functioning fairly well up until the end, but he was a changed man once he got a terminal diagnosis."

"And?"

She gave a broken laugh. "Bitter, angry, frustrated, depressed. I think his love turned to hate."

"I'm sorry," he said. "I guess that's the other side to a terminal illness a lot of people don't discuss. So often they can't make peace with dying. And take it out on those around them. Then there's that whole survivor-guilt thing."

She studied him for a long moment. "I hadn't considered that, but I guess that's partly what was going on."

Once again he turned and looked at her, his gaze direct but understanding. "Is that why you weren't happy at the end?"

She stared down at her hands. "If you'll be around town much, you'll hear the rumors, so I might as well tell you. He kind of went nuts. One of the things Charlie did in the last few months after the terminal diagnosis was particularly difficult." She took a deep breath before going on. "He decided he didn't want to miss out on anything anymore." Her voice fell silent.

He just waited until she could go on.

She took another deep breath, and this time shuddered a bit. "What he felt he'd missed out on was being with other women." She stared at Weston as she said it, watching his gaze widen. "That wasn't something I would have expected. I didn't find out right away. He was completely unapologetic when I did. So all these women around town he had his last hurrah with—it's mortifying. I ran into one at the grocery store this week. But there are at least half a dozen more."

"Wow," he said. "That's a pretty shitty deal."

"I think it was also his way of getting back at me," she said softly. "As a punishment for being healthy. Punishment for not dying, like he was." Her lips crooked up at the corner as she watched Weston shake his head in disbelief.

"I don't care what his damn reason was," he said. "Dying of cancer is terrible, I get that. But you don't have to drag everybody else through the muck just because you're on your way out."

"I never would have thought Charlie would be the kind to do that," she said, "so the betrayal was that much more shocking."

"And, of course, you stood by him the whole time, didn't you?"

"I didn't know what he was doing at first," she said. "And honestly, he'd gotten so unpredictable, it was easier when he was away from the house. Eventually it became clear it wouldn't be all that long before he was gone, or at least bedridden, and it was hard enough dealing with Sari and my own conflicting emotions, without having to figure out a way to move out and to get us set up again. We'd already moved once, when we had to sell the house we'd bought to pay for his treatments. In a way it all became a waiting game. And I hate to say it, but I was waiting for him to die."

"He didn't deserve you. The fact that you stuck by him is huge. I can't believe he did that to you."

"I'm no better," she said. "I stayed and kept the little we had left after the medical bills came out of the sales proceeds because I knew he wouldn't be here much longer. I'm not very proud of myself for that."

"You were married, so everything was yours together," he said. "He was dying, and he couldn't take anything with him. Even if you had moved out, no judge in the world would fight you over taking a few possessions. I presume you had wills?"

"Yes," she said. "And he left everything to me, just as my will left everything to him."

"Which is normal in a marriage, so I don't think he cared so much about making sure you didn't have anything at the end, as much as making sure he got to enjoy whatever time he had left for himself. Which is pretty selfish."

"Maybe selfish but, in some ways, understandable," she said softly. "It didn't do much for my self-confidence, or for my own grieving process, because it brought in a whole lot of other elements, including a wish he would die sooner, so I didn't have to deal with any more of his affairs."

"How many?"

"Eight that I know of," she said. "Maybe nine, if Angel isn't lying. Could be more. I don't want to know if there is. This has been hard enough."

"Jesus. That's horrible."

"More than horrible," she said, but she could feel a deep sigh rumbling through her ribs and up every neck bone before finally releasing.

He looked at her and smiled. "Maybe you needed to let that go too."

"Maybe," she said in a more cheerful voice. "I didn't realize how much I'd been hanging on to it. Something about Trudy chattering away her fake condolences at the grocery store the other day really bothered me, and I couldn't keep it to myself another minute. I actually called her out on it."

"I'm sorry I missed that," he said with a twitch of his lips. "I'm sure you created quite a scene."

"I'm not a scene-creating type of woman," she said sadly, "but I didn't have any self-control over it. I wanted Trudy to know I knew what she had done and that she was in good company with the rest of them, and I was more than happy to have everyone else in the store know it as well."

"Did you feel better afterward?" he asked curiously.

She tilted her head sideways, trying to remember. "I was pretty shaky and upset, but maybe I did. The only person to blame in all this was Charlie. But, at the same time, it took two to tango, and Trudy definitely had tangoed with Charlie. If she hadn't been so two-faced, I wouldn't have said anything. But, once she approached me, I let her have it. She is married too, by the way."

"Ouch."

"I know," she said. "I think that's one of the biggest things—you're taken for a fool, and everybody else is laughing behind your back at you."

"Trudy won't be laughing anymore," he said gently. "Or her poor husband. He probably ought to get a checkup."

That got a giggle out of her, which was what he was hoping for.

"Sometimes I feel like Charlie's up there, laughing at me, for the way he got to walk away from it all. He created all this chaos. He spent a ton of money at the end, which I could have used, and then he just happens to drive off the road."

"The whole thing was a real shit move on his part," he said. "It sounds like he was only about Charlie at the end, not about you and Sari at all."

"No, that's exactly what it was," she said. "It was pretty distressing to see how little he cared about us."

"I'm sorry," he said. "That's not an easy thing to deal with."

"No, it isn't. But I'm quite prepared to find a way to get past it all," she said. "It's just not that easy."

"No, none of this is easy," he said. "But you are a braver person than I am."

She laughed at that. "I don't think so."

"Oh, I do," he said. "Through all this you've maintained your same ethical and moral standards, and you've held your head high. You've done what's right, and you've looked after Sari at the same time. There isn't a whole lot more that can be asked of you."

WESTON THOUGHT ABOUT her words and the situation she'd gone through for the rest of the morning. It kept popping back up as he did research on the lawyer, on Angel, and on Ginger and Grant. Weston was no closer to finding any answers, and it was starting to irritate him. He stared out the window, wondering if he should just get out and take another look around Ginger's place. Not that it was likely to show him anything, particularly if Grant was there, but he wouldn't mind taking a better look at the crash site.

He doubted if the police had done much. A vehicle that's off the road can look like murder or an accident.

He sent the detective a text, asking for any updates, and got a fairly quick answer back, saying there was nothing. That just pissed off Weston more. He picked up the phone and called Badger. "Hey, any updates?"

"Yes," Badger said, his voice light. "I was just going to call you."

"Oh, what's up?"

"We paid for a rush on the DNA," he said. "Sari is definitely yours."

He sank back. He hadn't really wanted to consider it until he knew for sure; yet, at the same time, it was a huge relief. "Well, that's good to know," he said warmly, twisting to look down at the little girl. To think, she was actually his flesh and blood. And though he'd known it before, he hadn't really known it. Not like this.

"Does it change anything for you?"

"It just confirms what we had already hoped," he said. Sari was lying on her back playing with her toes, Shambhala right beside her. "Shambhala has definitely taken to her as well."

"That is a really good thing potentially," Badger said.

"Potentially," he said. "I'm just not so sure about the future."

"The future doesn't have to be secure right now either," Badger said. "Remember that. One day at a time."

"Did you have any luck tracking down Angel's whereabouts for the last eighteen months?"

"She worked in Vegas at one of the casinos for about six months. She lost her job and was at a different casino for another few months after that. She seemed to have a pattern of a job every couple months and then leaving."

"Any reason for why she left the jobs?"

"She was fired from the first one for drug abuse," he said, "and she's got a history of gambling, drugs and even prostitution."

Weston winced at that. "That sounds like a spiral that's

hard to get out of."

"I would say so. Yes."

"So I wonder what she's doing back up here," he asked.

"The only reason theoretically would be you and the baby," Badger said.

"She didn't know I was here, until I spoke to her on the phone recently, as she made one of her calls to Daniela," he said, as his fingers drummed the top of the table. "But then there's also the case of the murdered lawyer."

"Right. We're having trouble getting any cooperation from the police on that one."

"I'm not surprised. I sure would like to get into that law office though."

"We did access his computer files. Nothing suspicious is there, except for the fact there is no file on Sari."

As soon as Weston heard that, his heart sank. "Seriously?"

"Yes. If there was one, it's been deleted. Although I'm beginning to suspect there wasn't one."

"Like no digital copy but strictly a paper copy?"

"It's quite possible somebody other than the murderer could have deleted any digital materials," Badger said. "Somebody like Angel."

"So there would be no record of the adoption." Weston shook his head in disgust.

"It was registered in the US system though. According to the adoption registry, Sari officially belongs to Daniela."

"If that's the case, then she doesn't have anything to worry about," Weston said with a bright smile.

"Except for the fact that you're Sari's father, and you never signed away your rights. You could potentially have a claim on her."

"That's a different story," he said, "but it means Angel can't take her away, correct?"

"Unless she has a good sob story and can prove the baby's better off with her."

"That's terrible," he said. "Can't adoptive parents ever have the peace of mind of knowing someone can't come back on them?"

"It is definitely a confusing issue," Badger said. "Nothing's clear-cut these days. It's supposed to be finished, legal, all over, done with, but it never really is."

"You realize none of this makes any sense."

"It'll make sense," Badger said quietly. "Unfortunately it never makes sense until more shit happens." On that note he hung up.

Weston put down his cell phone and turned to look at his daughter.

"Who was that?" Daniela asked from the kitchen.

He looked up to see her leaning against the doorway, chewing on her bottom lip.

"The DNA came back," he said with a smile. "Sari is mine."

A look of happy surprise washed across her face. "That is excellent news," she said.

Sari looked over at him and gave him a toothy grin, then rolled back over, pushing at Shambhala with her feet as she lay on the floor.

"It is good news," he said quietly with a big smile on his face. "I hadn't realized how much I wondered until we got a confirmation."

"I'm sorry you had to wonder," she said. "Once Angel said you were the father, it never crossed my mind to think she might have been lying. Although, in retrospect, that wasn't very astute of me."

"Well, the reality is, she might not have known for sure," he said. He hopped to his feet and said, "I'll go into town and talk to the cops. I want to see if I can find out where Angel is staying, if she's even in town, and see if I can get any more information on her brother and all that."

"Did your friend have much to add?"

"Not much. Apparently Angel got into a spot of trouble in Vegas and ended up in drugs and eventually even prostitution. She went through a lot of jobs working at casinos. One lasted six months, and others were shorter."

"Ouch," Daniela said. "That would make for a tough eighteen months."

"Very," he said. "The problem is, we don't know what kind of a downward spiral she's come here with, and the truth is, we don't want her here at all."

"That's for sure."

He smiled. "I'll take Shambhala with me."

She hesitated and looked at Sari. "Okay. I'm still not all that comfortable with her here without you. Though it seems foolish to be uncertain because look at the two of them."

"I won't be too long anyway. We'll get out of your hair for a bit." He stopped as he headed toward the front door. "Do you want me to pick up anything while I'm out?"

She shook her head. "We'll be fine," she said. "I've got some work to do on my online business, and then I may have a nap with Sari. I didn't get a lot of sleep last night."

"If you think of anything," he said, "you can text me."

She nodded.

He called Shambhala, who hopped to her feet and came running. He laughed. "You're just as happy to get out and do something as I am, aren't you, girl?" He opened the front door and walked out to his rental truck.

He had a lot to think about, and not the least of which was what the hell he would do with his future. When he had been considering his future before, he had only himself in mind, not a family, but now he had a daughter. No way in hell he would let her out of his life on a permanent basis. The question really was, what did he want, and was it fair to even consider something other than 100 percent?

Weston loaded Shambhala into the vehicle and headed back into town, his mind full. Not getting answers wasn't good, and getting out of the house was more a case of staying busy. While he looked into these legal things, hopefully he could free up his mind and let all the thoughts and information flow through him.

He stopped in at the police station first.

The detective was there and looked surprised. "I told you that I didn't have any updates," he said.

"That may be," Weston said, "but I have news that Angel was into prostitution and drugs pretty heavily down in Vegas. I also know Daniela is really worried Angel will try to take custody back."

"I didn't think that was possible," the detective said. "I did send the paperwork to the legal department, but I haven't heard back yet."

"The adoption has been formally registered too," Weston said. "I just wondered if there was any chance Angel could upset the applecart and get Sari back."

"That I don't know," the detective said, then looked down at his files. "We haven't found anything helpful so far."

"So no forensic evidence?"

"Some, but that's classified."

Weston nodded. "Is the crime scene still locked up?"

"Why?"

"Because I'd like to take a look at the attorney's office," he said boldly. "I've done a lot of this kind of work in the past."

The detective studied him for a long moment, then making a sudden decision, he stood, grabbed his keys and said, "I'll meet you there."

"Good," Weston said, then strode out to his truck. Shambhala lay in the front seat, waiting for him. She barked in delight when he arrived, her tail wagging like crazy. He hopped in and reached over to give her a scratching.

"Let's go, girl, and see if we can get into trouble somewhere else." Starting the truck, he headed down the few blocks to the lawyer's office. He walked the block and took photos of the other offices in the same area. By the time he walked back, the detective frowned at him.

"What did that do for you?"

"It depends on if someone heard anything, saw anything," he said.

At that, the detective frowned. "We have spoken to several of the people in these nearby businesses, and nobody heard anything."

"Of course not. That's the way of it, isn't it?"

"Sometimes."

Weston held his thoughts to himself, but he wondered if anybody had seen Angel. Was there any strife with the lawyer? What kind of a person was he? These were all things he would take the time to find out. The detective unlocked the door and motioned inside.

Weston stepped in and stopped. "Did you guys make this mess?"

The detective stepped in behind him and frowned even more. "We shouldn't have," he said. "This isn't normal."

"It wasn't like this before," Weston said, as he turned in a slow circle. "All the files have been dumped upside down. Even if the killer were looking for something, why would you dump it like that?"

"Frustration? Rage?" The detective frowned as he pulled out his phone and calling forensics to see when they had been here last.

"The crime scene tape was down, correct?"

"Yes, the scene had been cleared."

"Do we know if this guy had any other relatives besides Angel?"

"I'm not sure," he said. "I haven't been working the case."

At that news, Weston just lifted an eyebrow. "Are there that many detectives here?"

"Yes and no," he said. "We've had two call in sick today."

Weston took a quick look around, wondering just what this was. To him it looked like rage. Somebody expected to find something, and, when they didn't, they decided to trash the place. Or they did find something, but it was something they didn't want to see.

He wondered what the lawyer was like. Was there any chance he was supposed to draw up the agreement and make sure it was not quite legal? That would be shitty on Angel's part.

But he didn't know what kind of a person she was. Unfortunately she was a ship that passed him in the night. They rocked the boat for a few hours, and that was it. He couldn't regret it now because Sari was the result, but it was certainly not something he even vaguely remembered. And that made him feel sad.

He squatted beside a stack of files on the ground. He didn't recognize any of the names. He didn't touch anything but continued to search through the material on the floor. Surely something was here. He found a pack of matches off to the side from a Vegas hotel. He studied it because it was of particular interest, since it was on top of the files. If it came from Angel, that meant she had been here, either before or after this destruction.

When the detective got off the phone, he had information. "The technicians were done yesterday. The crime scene tape was removed afterward, and the office was left locked."

Weston nodded, then pointed at the matches. "Angel lived and worked in Las Vegas," he said. "If those are from her, she's been here since this was done or was here at the time."

The cop squatted beside him and nodded. "What purpose would she have for searching through these records and leaving them in such a mess?"

Weston replied, "Either she was looking for something and couldn't find it, or she found something and didn't like it."

"Right," he said. "Well, I've got the team coming back, so make sure you don't touch anything."

"You know I won't." Weston walked through to the private office in the back, where he'd seen the body and saw bloodstains still on the carpet. He looked with a new insight because now all the information around this killing had changed.

"Do we know what the weapon was?" Weston asked.

"No, not for sure. A small handgun we assume. I'm still waiting for the autopsy to come back."

"So a gun that could be purchased almost anywhere," Weston said.

"There's more. The lawyer had a license himself and kept a gun on the premises. It's the same caliber he was killed with."

"Has it been found?"

"No," he said, "but it seems likely it may have been involved, one way or another."

"So somebody comes in here with ill intent. The lawyer pulls the gun to protect himself. Then they end up killing him with it?"

"It could play that way," the detective said. "Again, what's the motive?"

"Somebody wanted help," Weston said. "And either the lawyer didn't like it or didn't like the price."

"That sounds familiar," the detective said. "I was here for an hour after the body was removed, going through everything, but I didn't find anything of interest."

"So you didn't expect this aftermath?"

"No."

"Even now I don't see much point. An awful lot of case files are here, but depending on what he specialized in—"

"Mostly estates," the detective said. "We'll have to go through this paperwork, make sure nothing's missing. But we won't know on a lot of this if parts of the files are missing."

"So, like wills?" Weston said, turning to look at him.

The detective frowned and then nodded. "That's possible. He had a legal assistant, and I spoke with her yesterday. She wasn't sure what she was even supposed to do at this point."

"I'd like to talk to her."

"And what would you ask her?"

"I'd ask about any estates in the process of closing, and any clients or others who were disgruntled over a will."

"I did ask some of that but not all of it. Given this, I think more questioning needs to be done." The detective brought out a notepad and wrote down notes as he walked around the office, but Weston didn't bother too much about that.

"The next thing to question is, did this lawyer have anything to do with the wills for Grant and Ginger?"

The detective stopped, looked at him and said, "I have no idea." He pulled up his phone and started talking, "I think it's time I contacted that assistant again."

When a woman answered on the other end, he identified himself and told her the office had now been broken into, and paperwork was strewn everywhere. He said he needed to meet with her to go over a few more questions, but he also wondered if she could answer one right away.

As Weston listened with half an ear, he heard her acknowledge they had, indeed, done wills for Grant and Ginger. He nodded and said, "I'll come around this afternoon, and I'd like to show you some photos of the offices. I wonder if you'd feel up to helping us determine if anything is missing."

At that, Weston turned and asked, "Can she just come down here?"

The detective frowned. "Actually, would you mind running down here and taking a look? There are files everywhere." When he hung up the phone, he glared at Weston.

Weston held up his hands. "I know. I know. This is your case, not mine."

"Exactly," he said, "but it's a good idea to have her come and take a look. She should at least be able to say which ones were their current cases."

"And, if the office did handle Ginger and Grant's estate, in theory, this is now a connection to that case as well."

"He was a lawyer, and not too many were in this part of town," the detective said. "There could be a lot of different reasons for that connection."

"Possibly," Weston said cheerfully, "but it's better to have too much information than not enough."

"So says you," the detective said. "It's a fine line. Sometimes too much information clouds everything."

Weston had to agree.

Just then came a knock on the door, and it was pushed open, as a middle-aged woman stepped inside. "I'm Roseanne," she said. "The legal assistant." She stopped, took one look and gasped. "Oh my," she said, "all these files." She bent down to straighten them up and then stopped and looked at the detective. "May I?"

He shook his head. "Not yet. We'll have the forensic techs come back and take another look at this."

She frowned, noting some of the names and the open drawers.

Weston stepped forward and asked, "Did you utilize the files in this cabinet much?"

"No," she said. "Actually, we've been going digital, and we rarely used the paper files. Besides, that cabinet is old past clients."

"How old?"

"Well, last year anyway," she said. "Once we've crossed

over a year, we digitized any completed cases and got rid of the paper copies."

"So, these are all files from the last year that you haven't had a chance to digitize yet?"

"Yes," she said, "that's it exactly."

CHAPTER 15

DANIELA FOUND IT hard to settle after Weston left. Her mind was a little more than upset with everything going on, but this was more about what was upset inside herself. She was absolutely delighted to get confirmation that Sari was Weston's. That was good news. She wished to God that Angel wasn't the mother, but no amount of wishing would change that. And it wouldn't give Daniela her daughter either.

She was a mother in all but blood, but, for her, that was enough because she knew getting pregnant wasn't an option either. That was also why she was terrified of losing Sari.

Daniela decided she needed to spend some time out and about, instead of sitting at home, moping. She finished up a bit of work she had to do and then dressed Sari and took her to a popular play center. There they spent an hour and a half, toddling around with a couple other mothers. It was an enjoyable break from the norm of her crazy world and allowed her to step back from the heavy emotions. When she got a text from Weston, asking where she was, she called him instead.

"Hey," she said, "I'm at a play center with Sari. She's with two other little girls right now."

"Oh, great idea," he said. "Does she get along with other kids?"

He clearly asked the question out of a natural curiosity, so she didn't take offense. He hadn't been around little kids enough to know.

"She gets along famously with them." Looking at the other mothers, who were currently laughing and joking, she asked, "What are you up to?"

"Well, the lawyer's office was broken into," he said, "so we're here with the legal assistant, going over some of the cases, looking for something that may have triggered this kind of destruction."

"Good Lord," she said. "Is that the world you live in?"

"Very often, yes," he said. "I was just wondering if you wanted to go out for lunch."

"That would be lovely. I gather you haven't eaten?"

"No," he said. "I figured I might be too late, since it's past noon, but I thought I'd check."

"It's not too late," she said. "I'd love to. Where do you want to meet?" He mentioned a popular restaurant close by. "Perfect. Is fifteen minutes okay?"

"That works for me," he said cheerfully. After they hung up, she picked up Sari and said goodbye to the other moms.

Outside, Sari started talking. "Doggy, doggy."

"Yes," Daniela said. "We'll go see doggy." Then she frowned because, of course, Shambhala wouldn't be allowed in the restaurant. She wondered if Weston had even considered that. It was one thing to be a single guy and all of a sudden have a dog, but to have a dog, a daughter and the daughter's mother around would require some major adjustments, and she wondered if he was prepared.

But it was his problem, and one thing she did understand was that he was good at solving problems.

As they headed toward the restaurant, she pulled up to

the side of his rental truck to see Shambhala barking at them through the window. She held up Sari, who put her face and her palms against the glass, chattering away at Shambhala, who was wagging her tail frantically on the other side.

At that moment Weston stepped into sight. "I hope she'll be okay for an hour, but you're not making it easy on us."

Daniela rolled her eyes at him. "I couldn't get Sari past her. You know that."

"Good point," he said. He reached out his hands, and Sari surprised them both by reaching her arms back toward him. He swung her up into his arms. "Let's go eat, and then we'll come back and visit the doggy."

She cried out, "Doggy, doggy," over his shoulders.

As they went inside, he said, "Does she talk about anything else?"

"She does but not very often," Daniela said. "She's not behind or anything, but a first child is often a little bit slower to do some things than kids with older siblings in the home."

"She can be as slow as she wants to be," he said. "I'm not bothered."

And honestly he didn't appear to be, and that was very reassuring too. She smiled as they sat down at a table, specifically chosen where they could look out and see Shambhala still in the truck.

"You've taken on quite a few encumbrances all of a sudden," she pointed out.

He looked at her in surprise, then glanced down at his daughter and back over at the dog. He gave a wide shoulder shrug. "It doesn't matter," he said. "I'm actually enjoying it."

"Sure, but it's not something that you just enjoy and then stop."

He looked at her gently. "I'm not planning on running away."

"I get that." She felt awkward, but she didn't quite know what else to say, so she focused on the menu instead. "Everything sounds delicious."

He smiled. "Get whatever you want."

She looked at him, not sure if he was treating her or if she was paying. If she was paying, the budget definitely came into play.

When the waitress came back, he ordered a burger and fries, then looked at Daniela. "What will Sari eat?"

Daniela ordered chicken fingers and fries and then a salad for herself. "Sari and I can share," she said.

He chuckled at that. "Meaning, you get to clean up her leftovers?"

She shrugged. "I'm not too sure too many mothers out there don't," she confessed.

"You can have food just for yourself too, you know?"

"I'm happy this way." From his frown she wasn't sure he believed her, but he didn't make an issue of it. When the food arrived, the salad was way better than she had expected. And she did share it with Sari because Sari loved salads. She wasn't a big eater anyway, so, by the time she'd had several bites of salad, a couple chicken fingers and fries, she was more than done and wanted to go back to the doggy. When Daniela was done with her salad, she put down her fork.

"What are your plans for this afternoon? Do you have a babysitter?" Weston asked suddenly.

She frowned at him and looked down at Sari. "Why?"

"I'd like to take you out for dinner," he said. "A real date."

Immediately heat flushed through her. She smiled and

knew her cheeks were turning pink. "Well, that would be very nice," she said, "but I'm not too sure if it's a good idea."

"It might not be, or maybe it is," he said, "but we'll never know if we don't try. Do you have a babysitter?"

"My sister sometimes will take Sari."

"Will you call her and see if that's an option?"

"She's never looked after her in the evening before," Daniela said, chewing on her bottom lip.

"We could take Sari over there and then pick her up after dinner," he said, "or your sister could come to the house."

Daniela pulled out her phone and sent her sister a text. When the response came back. neither a yes nor no but a why, she sighed, and said, "She wants to know why."

"Of course she does," he said. "So tell her."

She looked at him for a moment.

Weston said, "Unless you're ashamed of me."

"Of course I'm not," she said, frowning. She texted back that Weston had invited her out on a date.

Her phone rang, and she rolled her eyes at Weston. "This is why you don't tell my sister these things. She always wants more details." She answered the phone. "Hello, sis."

"Is that a good idea?" her sister demanded. Daniela reached up and pinched the bridge of her nose, then said, "That's one of the reasons we would like to go out on a date. So we can figure out if it's a good idea," she said gently.

A humming sound came on the other end of the phone. "What time?"

She looked at Weston. "What time?"

"Seven?" he said. "I'll make reservations at a local restaurant, if that's okay with you."

"That sounds lovely," she said to Weston, but to her sister she added, "So seven to nine?"

At that, Davida said, "Fine, I'll come over and be there at quarter to seven."

"Good enough," she said. "And thanks, sis."

"I just want to see this guy again," Davida said. "I'm not sure about him." Then she hung up.

With a heavy sigh Daniela faced Weston. "She's agreed to seven to nine."

"Perfect," he said. "Do you have a favorite restaurant?"

She thought about it, then shook her head. "I didn't go out much with Charlie."

"Good," he said. "We'll find someplace new."

She chuckled. "Is it that easy?"

"It's definitely that easy," he said with a smile.

She shrugged and said, "Well then, you pick a place, and I'll be happy to go."

"Is there any food in particular that you don't like?"

"No, I don't think so," she said. "I eat seafood and basically everything really."

"Good to know," he said.

She smiled at him. "If you're sure."

"I'm sure," he said, then looked at his watch. "I'll pay the bill, and then I'll leave you two to head off and do whatever you do on a girls' afternoon."

As he stood, pulling money from his wallet, he checked the bill, then leaned over and kissed Sari on the cheek, making her giggle. Then he leaned over and kissed Daniela on the cheek as well. "I'll be home well in advance of our date tonight." And, with that, he was gone.

She stared after him, bemused as he headed to the vehicle. He was greeted excitedly by Shambhala and then drove away. She looked back at Sari to see her staring at her wide-eyed, her fingers on her cheek where she'd been kissed.

Daniela leaned forward and whispered, "I know, right?" Then she reached up and touched the spot on her own cheek where she'd received a matching kiss. "Pretty darn special."

And Sari chortled in glee.

WESTON DIDN'T REALLY have plans, but just so much was going on that he needed to stir up some more information before this slipped away and became a cold case. He knew he was really pushing it, and he trusted the detective to do what he could, but obviously they were short-staffed. He headed back to the lawyer's office, surprised to see forensics there already. He went to the other businesses and introduced himself, then explained why he was there and asked if they had known the lawyer.

One woman at the front desk of an insurance company nodded. "He was a great guy," she said warmly. "We were really devastated to learn of his death."

"You didn't hear anything I presume?"

She shook her head. "Nothing. I don't remember seeing him this week at all. Some days we don't. He's busy, arriving early and nearly always leaving well after I do," she said.

He nodded and smiled, then asked a few more questions, but there didn't seem to be anything to add. He went up and down all the businesses in the block and got largely the same report: that the lawyer was a good guy and that nobody had any idea why someone would have shot him.

Now to come back to this whole Grant and Ginger thing. He realized he may need to have another talk with Grant—or whoever he was. It was possible he was Gregory, but Weston really had no idea. He was a little on the fence about it. He headed back into the vehicle with Shambhala, letting her up first, noting again how well she jumped, at least for now.

He checked the time and found it was only two-thirty, so he headed down the road out to the homestead. He pulled off the side of the road at the site of the accident, and, with Shambhala on a leash, he hiked down to where the crash site was. The wrecked vehicle was still there, and he suspected that budgetary limitations may have prevented it from being hauled out. They had taken the two bodies from the vehicle, but that was it.

Shambhala barked and jumped around at the bottom, but she didn't seem to exhibit any signs that this was where she'd been tossed or where her owners had died. It was in complete contrast to their first visit. Maybe the dog had figured out that her beloved owner was gone now, and she was okay to move on. Animals did adjust faster than humans ...

He walked around the crushed-in truck. It had flipped and rolled several times and had landed on its wheels, at an angle, so it was tilted upward, not quite sideways, but lodged in between a couple rocks at a forty-five-degree angle. The hood was crushed flat, and the bed was pretty damaged with the sides caved in.

He couldn't tell from the damage on the vehicle if there'd been any foul play. And, of course, on a stretch of road like this, it was pretty easy for accidents to happen, so it was totally within reason that it had been an accident, just as it appeared. But who was to say for sure? It was just one more in a pile of unknowns he had no answers for.

He got a door open and peered inside. Almost nothing was left, since a fire had scorched the interior as well. He stared at the cliff up above. Looking at Shambhala, he muttered, "Be pretty hard to survive that. Plus with the fire afterward."

He shook his head and started the slow climb back up. Just as he neared the steepest part of the climb, a single gunshot rang out. He ducked, reacting by instinct and pulling Shambhala with him back behind the brush. He swore softly as the dog curled up close to his side, whimpering. He hugged her close. "I know. We never wanted to hear that again, did we?"

Her tail thumped in response, but she kept her trembling body against him.

"But here we are, girl, so we'll have to deal with it. Let's hope they don't get a chance for a second shot."

He waited for a long moment to see if anybody would come looking for them. When he heard no movement, he picked up a rock and threw it down closer to the vehicle, causing a few other rocks to move down. Instantly a second shot was fired. Swearing, he pulled out his phone and sent Badger a message, then sent Detective Kruger a message as well. When the detective texted back, Weston was told to stay undercover, and the detective was on the way.

Weston snorted at that. "I could be dead before you get here," he snapped as he peered through the brush, trying to see who the shooter was. The shots came from the other side of the road, toward Grant's homestead, but that didn't mean it was him. Or Gregory. Weston hadn't seen a vehicle when he drove up, and they were still a good many miles away from the cabin, so there was no logical reason to assume it was one of the twins. Neither would have known Weston was even driving out this way. Unless, of course, one of them had been tracking him.

He frowned at that. It was one thing for his military buddies to have access to tracking equipment, but it was not common for someone like Grant. Then again, Weston didn't know what his history was, and maybe he needed to check that. He sent another text to Badger, asking if anybody in Grant's family had a military or law enforcement background. He couldn't be sure it was him shooting, but the only way the shooter would know Weston was here was if his vehicle had been tracked. Badger said he'd look into it but also told Weston to check for a tracker when he got back to his vehicle.

He sent back a simple text. **You think?**

It was interesting that Badger didn't have any expectation of him doing anything but getting safely back to his truck because that was what they did. Survive.

CHAPTER 16

D ANIELA COULDN'T KEEP the smile off her face for the rest of the afternoon. Back home, she had a shower, washed her hair and couldn't believe how excited she was at the thought of going out on a date. She went through half-a-dozen outfits in her closet before finally settling on a simple dress and heels. It was nice and summery, and she could wear it with a sweater or even a nice jacket to head off the evening's chill. Satisfied with that, she hung it up on the outside of the closet, and, with her hair wrapped in a towel, and Sari at her feet, playing with her scarves, Daniela set about doing a quick facial mask. When her phone rang, her face was covered in gunk, but she laughed and picked up the phone anyway. "Hello?"

"I want my daughter back," Angel said.

"She's my daughter," Daniela said calmly, though inside, her heart slammed against her ribs. "It's all legal and above-board, Angel. You don't get any callbacks on this one."

"You say it's all legal," she said, "but I know my brother. He was a lousy lawyer. I'm sure he missed something."

"I don't think so. Did you kill your brother because he wouldn't help you get Sari back?"

Nothing but silence came on the other end of the phone. Then Angel snapped, "You don't have a clue what you're talking about."

"No, maybe not, but I'll defend my daughter to the death," she said. "Just remember. She's my daughter, not yours. You gave up all rights to her." She didn't know where her bravado came from; she just knew how important it was that she maintain it.

"That's not fair," Angel said. "I didn't know what I was doing."

"No. You did know. That's the thing. Back then you knew exactly what you were doing and couldn't get it done fast enough. The sad part is, for whatever reason, you've come back to try to change it now. But, Angel, despite what you say, I don't believe for one minute it has anything to do with your maternal instincts or your concern for Sari's best interests."

"I need her," Angel said, and a certain amount of urgency was evident in her voice.

Frowning, Daniela said, "What for?"

"You wouldn't understand," she said, "but I have to have her."

"No. She is not a pawn for whatever game you're playing." With that, Daniela hung up.

Shaking, her hands trembling badly, she dropped the phone on the bed and sank down beside Sari. Knowing she might scare her little girl, Daniela resisted the temptation to hug her and just curled around Sari and watched while she played with the scarves, rolling around and laughing. Daniela didn't know what she'd do if anything happened to little Sari.

Daniela's heart was completely overwhelmed with the idea of Angel being a threat. It never occurred to her at the time of the adoption that something like this would happen. Of course it should have. She must have had at least some inkling that Angel wasn't completely stable. It was one of the reasons why they'd been happy to pay for Angel's flight to Vegas, just to get her out of Alaska.

But now Angel was back.

Daniela had promised to let Weston know if she heard from Angel, so she picked up her phone and called him. When he answered, his voice was distracted.

"I just heard from Angel again," she said. "She said she *needs* Sari. Not that she loves her or misses her or anything like that. Just that she needs her and that I wouldn't understand."

An odd silence came on the other end before he said, "Make sure you stay inside with the doors locked, okay?"

"Okay," she said, "but now you're scaring me. Why?"

"Listen. Don't panic, but I'm pinned at Ginger's accident site. Somebody is shooting at me," he said. "I don't know what the hell Angel is doing, but I'm not in a position to head that way just yet. But you call me if there's even a hint of trouble. If somebody tries to steal my daughter, I will be there no matter what," he said.

"Oh, my God, Weston," she said. "Are you okay?"

"Yeah," he said with a broken laugh. "I'm fine. Shambhala's here too, and we're both fine. I'm just waiting for him to disappear or to come after me."

"Why would you say that?" she asked.

"Well, because it's got to stop," he said. "So this guy has to come to see if he's taken me out, which is a dangerous move, or else he'll retreat. But then he won't know for sure."

"You have no idea who it is?"

"No," he said. "I'm at the accident site where Ginger and supposedly Grant died. I was just coming up the hill to get back to the truck when somebody started shooting."

"And you think it's Grant or his brother?"

"I have no clue," he said, "but I don't want to miss anything here, so I'll get off the phone now. Go lock up the doors and windows, then stay put. I'll check in soon." With that, he hung up.

She went downstairs to lock the front door. As she checked the windows, she wondered if she should just cancel the date tonight. Safety was paramount, and she didn't want to put her sister in a difficult situation either. She hesitated making the call, thinking she would give it some time, see what would happen.

Just twenty minutes later, her phone rang. She snatched her phone, hearing Weston's voice as soon as she picked it up. "Are you okay?"

"I'm fine," he said in a cheerful voice. "The guy's gone."

"But that means you don't know who it was, right?"

"No, but the detective is here. We're taking fingerprints off my rented vehicle. I looked for but didn't find a tracker. We found where he was shooting from and tracked his footprints too, so we're better off than if he hadn't shot at me."

She sat down hard in the kitchen chair. 'That sounds crazy. I don't understand how this all started."

"I'm not sure either," he said. "I'm heading out to Grant and Ginger's now, with the detective. Don't worry. I still expect to be home on time for our dinner date."

"Earlier you made it sound like you thought Sari and I were in danger. Should we even be going out tonight?"

He hesitated and then said, "Or, we could take Sari to your sister's house and pick her up on the way home. Would that be better?"

"It would probably make me feel better. I wouldn't want

to put my sister in danger."

"Understood," he said. "So call your sister and see if that'll work for her."

"Or we could just do it later," she said, fretting.

"You can't keep avoiding us," he said.

"Avoiding what?" she asked. "I haven't been on a date in years, so what difference does it make if I wait a little longer?"

"I hear you," he said. "But I really would like to spend some time with you."

"We could pick up and bring it in?" she said hopefully.

He laughed. "Are you afraid of me or afraid of going out on a date?"

"Neither. I'm afraid of something happening when we're not here. I would never forgive myself."

"Fine," he said. "I'll pick up something and bring it home. But I'm not counting that as the date. We're just pushing that back a bit."

"That's fine," she said. "Once this craziness is over, we won't have to worry so much."

"Maybe not as much as now," he said, "but I doubt if it'll be over that quickly."

She frowned at that. "So, do you know when you'll be home?"

"A couple hours," he said. "Go ahead and call your sister and cancel. But remember. It's a temporary postponement." With that, he hung up.

THE DETECTIVE DROVE in front of him, and, with Shambhala beside him, Weston drove his rental right through to Grant and Ginger's property. When Weston hopped out, the detective stood on the front porch, knocking on the door. No vehicles were around, no signs of life. When there was no response from inside, the detective pushed open the door as it was already slightly ajar. With Shambhala at his side, Weston caught up and the two walked into the living room.

"Hello? Anyone home?" Weston called out.

Shambhala headed for her bed in front of the fireplace and lay down.

He looked at her and smiled. "Every time we come here, she goes there."

"Smart dog," the detective said. "But where the hell is Grant?"

"Do you believe it's Grant, or do you think it's his brother, Gregory?"

"I have no clue. I don't particularly like either of them, and nothing about this situation makes any sense."

"I hear you there," Weston said.

They did a quick search of the cabin but found nobody here.

Weston walked over to the fridge and pulled it open. "Doesn't look like the guy's been staying here," he said, "because the fridge is empty."

They checked everything else, but it didn't look like anybody was living here at all.

"If it *is* Grant," the detective said, "why wouldn't he stay here? It's his place."

"Looks like we're back to that same issue."

"I don't like anything about this." Frustrated, the detective stood in the center of the living room, turning around in a slow circle.

"And what does that threatening letter have to do with anything?" Weston asked, leaning against the sink, his arms across his chest. "And the shooter?" he added. "Where the hell did he come from?"

"It makes sense that it would have been Grant or Gregory. I just don't know why."

"And did it have anything to do with the lawyer who handled the Buckmans' estate?"

"That's another question," the detective said. "We've got people going through the dead lawyer's files to see if anything unusual is in there. But the Buckman estate hasn't been settled yet because it's only been six weeks. Everything goes to the brother though, so that shouldn't have been much of an issue."

"No. Unless somebody else was supposed to get it."

The detective raised both hands, palms up. "So, what? He kills the two of them, expecting to get the property? We don't have anybody else here to blame."

"How old was Ginger?"

The detective smirked. "She was coming up on her fifties. Her husband was a little younger."

"She was a looker?"

He frowned at that. "Yes, she was. Like one of those women who never really ages. She used to be a model or some such thing. I don't know."

"Interesting," Weston said.

"Why? What are you thinking?"

"How old do you think Grant is?"

"He was younger for sure," the detective said. "Maybe forty, or almost anyway."

"Right. Any chance Ginger's kids are after the property? Like maybe they figured that the couple was dead, and they should get it instead of Gregory?" Weston headed out to the front door, around the porch. He thought he'd heard something but wasn't sure. He didn't have a weapon, but he did have Shambhala, and her ears were pointed toward the woodshed. He looked back at the detective and lifted a finger to his lips. With Shambhala at his side, he headed there.

He walked around the outside perimeter of the outbuilding first, and then he pulled the door wide open but hid behind it, in case any shots were fired. No sound came. Ears up, Shambhala stared around the corner, but they didn't hear another sound.

Shrugging, he went inside. The woodshed was heavily packed for the winter, which was a good sign. There was a space at the far end for some tools and for access, but not a ton of openings for someone to hide in. Then again, it didn't take a lot.

As his eyes became accustomed to the darkness, he heard the detective coming up behind him. He turned to look just as a rifle barrel came down from the top of the woodshed, where somebody had obviously been hiding. Reaching up, Weston grabbed the rifle barrel before it could fire and swung it to the ground, along with the shooter.

The detective pounced on him, and, sure enough, it was Grant. "Now what the hell are you up to?"

He spat on the ground. "You're trespassing."

"You're a dead man," Weston said carelessly.

Shambhala once again sat at Weston's side but didn't appear to want to go toward the man. Weston already knew Shambhala preferred Ginger to Grant, but still, most dogs had a relationship with both people in a situation like this. Shambhala could still prefer one but be friendly to both.

He looked at her and frowned. "Shambhala, you don't

seem to care about this guy."

"Best evidence I've seen yet to say it's not Grant," the detective said. "My money says it's the bloody brother."

"Even if I am, what difference does it make?"

"It doesn't. The place is probably yours once probate is done," the detective said.

"Unless you killed to get it," Weston said.

"I didn't kill anybody," he said.

"Somebody's got to know if this is Gregory or Grant," Weston said.

"Maybe, maybe not," the guy said. "Maybe you're just being fooled."

At that, the detective stopped and said, "Are there just the two brothers?"

"I don't know," he said with a big grin.

Because he was being an asshole, Weston wanted to punch him for the sake of punching him. "Why don't you charge him with murder one," he said to the detective. "It's obvious he ran his brother and his wife off the road anyway."

The detective looked at him in surprise, then looked back at the man and frowned. "Did you?"

"Hell no," he said. "What would be my motive?"

"This place," Weston said.

"What about this place? Nothing's here."

"What were you doing in the woodshed?" Weston said, changing the subject.

"None of your fucking business."

"What are you looking for on the property?" he asked. At that, the man stiffened, and Weston knew he was on the right track. "What did they do? Find a gold claim or something?"

"Were they running some other business, and you found

out and came to help yourself?" the detective added.

"You don't know anything," he said with a sneer.

"No, I don't," the detective said, "but I know two people are dead, and you're the hand behind it."

"I am not." He turned to look at the detective. "You've got nothing on me."

The detective looked at Weston with a frown.

Weston said, "Take a sample of his handwriting and match it up against the threatening letter."

"Oh, shit," the detective said. "You know what? I've been really worn out, working with half my team gone. Otherwise I would have picked it up sooner. You're the one who threatened them, aren't you?"

"And what did you do, cut the brake lines or something?" Weston asked.

"Under the circumstances, nobody looked hard for forensic evidence because the vehicle was so badly smashed and burned," the detective added.

"Which explains why this guy here, with his rifle, was shooting at me earlier today when I got to nosing around the accident vehicle."

The man just glared at both of them.

"We still don't know if you're Grant or Gregory," Weston said. "I've been asking around town to see if one of you had any distinguishing marks, but, outside of a couple broken bones and whatnot, it doesn't seem there's a whole lot of difference. The X-rays will sort it out though."

At that, the man before them frowned, as if trying to recall what breaks they were talking about.

"We can surely get a warrant to have him X-rayed, can't we?" Weston asked the detective.

"Yep. For suspicion of murder, we can. I still don't understand what his motivation was," the detective said. "There is this place, but it won't fetch a whole lot of money."

"Not sure it was even about money as much as a place to disappear."

"You don't even know who I am," he said. "Until you do, you've got no motive, and you'll never get a warrant."

"Maybe," Weston said, turning to study the area. "But we'll find it if we start digging."

"No, you won't," he said.

Just then Weston's phone buzzed. It was Badger. He looked at the message. "Oh, look at that. Gregory's got a record in Las Vegas for cheating, stealing, not to mention, breaking and entering." Weston whistled. "And look at this—suspicion of manslaughter." He glared at the guy. "You got yourself in a shit ton of trouble, didn't you?" He turned to the detective. "You better get those files out of Las Vegas pretty damn fast, I'd say. Guess we won't need the X-rays after all. This guy's been fingerprinted plenty of times."

The detective turned to look at the man. "That's it. I'm taking you in for questioning."

"I'm not going," the guy said, stepping back. "I'm not the one responsible for all that shit."

"So you're either Gregory or you are Grant then, and we'll know the truth sooner or later."

"Crap," he said, and he seemed to sag in place.

However, that was just a decoy because, as the detective turned and relaxed, the man pulled out a handgun from his back waistband and held it on Kruger.

"Whoa, son, take it easy now," the detective said, backing out.

"I won't take it easy. That's my brother who died down there, but he didn't die hard enough. He brought that shithole of a loan shark up here with him. They've been hassling us for a long time, but, no, my brother wasn't happy enough with that, he had to go and get my bloody wife pregnant too, didn't he?"

"I have no idea. Did he? Do we need to do an autopsy on her and find out for sure?"

"There shouldn't have been any more than a few crispy critters left after that fire," he said. "But the damn thing wouldn't even burn on its own. I had to go down there and light it on fire."

"Why? Because he was screwing your wife? Did you really hate your wife that much?"

"Nobody likes to be made a fool of like that," he said. "What I told you in the first place was true. What I didn't tell you is that my brother came here, in trouble, but he also brought the trouble with him. Some guy he owed money to—a loan shark—came up behind him. Him and his muscle threatened me, and they threatened her. When we realized it was all about Gregory, he was laughing like a loon, thinking it was funnier than shit. I made a deal with a loan shark that he could have my brother, but he was to go away and leave us alone. I haven't got anything left," he said.

"Well, you could have gotten some help for that," Weston said, studying him closely. He couldn't see a killer in him as much as a man who had been pushed to the wall. But he was a killer nonetheless, particularly since he had a handgun in his hand.

"I just couldn't take it anymore, and I shot Gregory," he said. "As I stood there, staring down at the body, my wife came down the stairs and started screaming at me, telling me how she loved him, and he was the father of her child. She just wouldn't stop. I turned the handgun around, and I started wailing on her, and all of a sudden I had two bodies on the floor. She wasn't dead, but she might as well have been, so I loaded them up and drove them over to the edge. Took the dog with me thinking to kill her too, just clean the slate. But she jumped out and took off. I put my brother in position and pushed the whole mess over the cliff. I knew it was so far down that nobody would bother trying to get it back up again. But the damn thing wouldn't even burst into flames, though I'd figured it would for sure. So then I had to climb down and light it on fire." He sagged in place but kept the gun ready. "It's not the way I wanted things, and I loved my wife, but I just couldn't stand the thought of her having an affair with him."

"So she did know it was him then?" Weston asked to clarify Grant's earlier story.

He nodded. "I wanted to believe she didn't know, but there was no way I could, when she blurted it all out."

"Right. Well, son, you got a pile of trouble on your hands," the detective said.

"You're not kidding," he said, "and then that stupid bitch showed up."

"What bitch? Your wife?"

"No, the one who was with the loan shark. Both of them out of Vegas," he said. "She said she could score up here too. But then something happened between her and the loan shark, and he up and left her behind."

"Are you talking about Angel?" Weston asked, dumb-founded.

Grant looked over at him and frowned. "Yeah, Angel. What do you know about her?"

"I know she's nothing but trouble," he said. "Any idea what she's doing here?"

"No. Something about a baby, but she didn't look like she gave a shit about the kid, just that she had a deal going."

"Sounds like something Angel would try," Weston said, disgusted.

"I don't know," Grant said, "she was kind of unnerving." He looked over at the sheriff. "I can't stay here in hiding forever," he said. "You might as well take me in."

"I'd like to," he said, "but you're the one holding the handgun."

"I know," Grant said. "A lifetime locked up or eat a bullet."

"Don't eat a bullet," Weston said. "There's always another answer." Then another loose thread surfaced in his mind. "Was that you taking potshots at me earlier?"

"Yeah, too bad I missed. However, I could kill two more," he said, looking at the men before him, as if contemplating it. The detective shook his head. "And then you'll just get hunted down, and you lose your home anyway."

"It's gone already," he said. "Apparently my bloody brother and my lovely wife mortgaged the hell out of it and took the money. Paid the loan shark, and he's gone, but now I've got nothing but a massive mortgage."

The longer he talked, the more he stared at the gun. Weston was afraid he would do something serious about all this. That was not how Weston wanted this to end, but unfortunately he had no way to know if that was on Grant's mind or not. He just didn't trust him.

"There's always another answer," Weston said in a calm voice. "I'm sorry that things turned out the way they did, but—"

"Not for me," Grant said, as he fired a single shot.

CHAPTER 17

WHEN WESTON WALKED up to the front door, the look on his face had Daniela racing toward him. She came to a stop about four feet away, her eyes round and her hand going to her mouth.

He held a finger to his lips and said quietly, "I'll go have a shower."

She nodded mutely, studying the bloodstains all over his shirt. She swallowed hard. "Is any of that blood yours?"

He gave her a small grin and shook his head. "No. It's Grant's."

Her shoulders sagged with relief. "Did you have to kill him?"

"No," he said, "but, once we had him cornered with the truth, he ended up blowing apart his own head."

Her mind flashed on the image. "Well, as much as I'm glad it's not you, I'm sorry you had to see that."

He acknowledged her concern with a nod, followed by a shrug that only partially hid the pain. "I've seen it before," he said. "Unfortunately war leaves us with images we can never get rid of." And, with that, he took the stairs two at a time to get out of sight before Sari saw him. Daniela appreciated his concern, although, at her age, Sari probably wouldn't understand what the blood was anyway. It was more the pain in his eyes that bothered her.

Just as she headed back to Sari, her phone rang. It was her sister.

"Are you sure you want to cancel?" she asked. "I was thinking about it earlier, and I've been pretty rough on you. Maybe if you did spend time with him alone, you would see he isn't what you want."

At that, Daniela rolled her eyes. "I get that you don't want me to have a boyfriend," she said, "but I'm not at all sure that's the role he would take."

"I didn't say that," her sister protested. "It's just not been all that long."

"It was well over a year with a cheating, lying husband at the end, who I nursed out of duty rather than love," she said. "Exactly how long do I have to wait before I'm happy?"

Silence. "I'm sorry," Davida said in little more than a whisper. "You're right, and, if you do decide to go out tonight, let me know. I would be more than happy to come over." And she hung up.

But, after seeing the look in Weston's eyes and the blood on his clothes, Daniela didn't think that going out tonight was the best idea. And considering Angel was still a problem made it a worse idea.

Instead, since Weston hadn't brought anything home, and Shambhala had already found Sari in the playroom, Daniela searched in her fridge, looking for something to make for dinner. They'd had restaurant food for lunch, so they probably didn't need anything terribly heavy. She stared at the contents of her freezer, looking for inspiration, when Weston walked into the kitchen, tucking a clean shirt into his jeans.

"Sorry I didn't bring anything. I'd be happy to order in or go pick something up."

"How do you feel about pasta?" she asked, pulling out a pack of sausages.

"Sausages and pasta?"

She laughed. "You don't have to say it like that. It's really good. Trust me."

"If you're up for cooking," he said, "I'm up for eating. But it's not how I envisioned the evening to be."

She waved that off. "Let's do that another day," she said with a smile. She stopped and studied him carefully. "How are you doing?"

He didn't make any pretense of trying to ignore her, but he nodded and said, "I'll be fine. It always takes a little bit to detach from something like that."

She nodded and popped the sausages into the microwave to defrost, so she could slice them. Then she said, "I don't know if you're a hugger or not, but if you could use a hug—"

Instantly he opened his arms. She looked at him in surprise, then stepped into the embrace. But it seemed like he was offering her as much comfort as she was giving him. When he wrapped his arms around her and tucked her in closer, she melted against him. It was just so nice to be held by somebody who cared.

When he finally released her, he said, "Thank you."

She looked up at him, startled, having forgotten the reason she had offered him the hug in the first place. Then she smiled. "You're welcome," she said, as she kissed him gently on the cheek. Then she went back to bustling in the kitchen.

He sat down at the island. "Can I help?"

She thought about it a moment, then nodded and gave him several tomatoes, a cutting board and a knife. "Dice them up small please, like bite-size."

He went straight to work, and then she gave him some pickled artichoke hearts. His eyebrows popped up, but he kept slicing.

Then she gave him a can of large black olives and said, "These are big, so maybe give them a chop too." In the meantime, she had a pot of water boiling for pasta, and the sausage slices were simmering in a skillet nearby.

He looked at it all with interest. "I've never had something like this. It looks interesting."

She shrugged. "It's one of my favorites." She walked to the fridge, pulled out feta cheese and gave him the big square and said, "Cut off about a one-inch slab and cut it into small cubes."

He did as she instructed, while she pulled out some dishes.

She efficiently drained the corkscrew pasta, then put them into a bowl with butter, added salt and pepper and squeezed lemon juice on top. He stared at her in surprise, and she just chuckled and reassured him once more. Moving the bowl closer to the stove, she tossed in the cooked sausage pieces, including the fat left in the pan. Next she tossed in all of the vegetables he'd chopped, put the cheese on top and when it was all mixed up, she served dishes for the three of them.

"If you want to grab Sari," she said, "we can eat on the patio. I've got all three bowls."

Together they headed to the outside table. Weston snagged the high chair on the way out with his spare hand, and setting it at the table, gently plopped Sari in her chair.

She looked at the pasta and laughed with both hands outstretched. Her bowl was plastic, and, with an inquiring eye at Daniela for approval, Weston gave Sari the whole bowl. She went for the noodles and started chewing away.

"She does love to eat, doesn't she?" Taking a bite from his own bowl, he stopped in surprise as the flavors melded in his mouth. "Wow."

"Like I said, it's a favorite of mine," Daniela said. "It's supereasy and fast, but good."

"You're not kidding," he said. "I could eat this anytime." As it was, he inhaled his bowl, then went back inside and brought the big bowl back out with him and had seconds.

Minutes later, as he pushed away his empty bowl, he said, "You know something? As much as I would have liked to have taken you out for dinner, this was delicious."

She smiled at him, pleased with the compliment. "Good," she said. "Sometimes a home-cooked meal hits the spot."

"And sometimes going out is fun and a much-deserved break from cooking," he said.

She nodded. "So, do you want to tell me what happened today?"

"Hard to even know where to start," he said, "but I must because some of it involves Angel."

At that, Daniela's stomach twisted. She pushed away her dishes, grabbed his hand and said, "Tell me, please."

He cupped both of her hands and then gently rubbed them. Sari was happily chewing away on her pasta beside them, and Shambhala had quietly taken up residence below her for any food that fell off Sari's high chair. He half suspected Sari was deliberately dropping some for her. But nothing was in their dinner the dog couldn't eat and having Sari happily distracted right now wasn't a bad thing. He explained what had happened throughout the day, and then, when he told her about the loan shark coming up from

Vegas, Daniela gasped in surprise.

"Would they do that?"

"If there's money to be had, sure. Apparently Grant and his wife had pooled a little money, and the twin brother, Gregory, knew about it. He came up here but changed his plans at some point and decided to leave Grant holding the bag with the loan shark, while he took off with Ginger."

She winced at that. "Wow, after they took all the money, I suppose?" she said caustically.

He nodded. "Ultimately the loan shark got paid and left. Grant's brother and his wife are dead, and Grant was sitting there, trying to figure out how to rebuild his life now that the homestead is mortgaged to the hilt. He finally did admit to having killed both of them and tried to hide it by staging the accident. He pushed the truck over the edge with them in it, and, after it didn't blow up and burn on its own, he went down and torched it."

Her jaw dropped open.

Weston nodded. "It's always surprising to see the extent people will go to in order to get what they want."

"Yeah. And Angel? How did she fit into your busy day?" she asked, bewildered.

"Get this. Apparently she owed the loan shark something too, though I don't quite understand all that yet. Grant didn't have the details but said she'd arrived with the loan shark and made reference to an opportunity for a payout here. Something to do with a baby."

Instinctively she turned and looked at Sari; then her horrified gaze flipped back at him.

He nodded. "I just don't know exactly what that means yet."

"She wouldn't kidnap Sari, would she?"

"I hope not," he said grimly. "The bottom line is, we're not letting her have Sari."

"But, if she did, what would she do with her?"

Weston had some really ugly ideas about that because he'd seen the ugly side of people too much in his life, but he didn't want to say anything to Daniela.

"She would sell her, wouldn't she?" Daniela said, clearly outraged.

"Until we find her, we don't know. The detective had to bring the forensic team out to Grant's place, and Kruger's put out an APB for Angel. We could hope she's disappeared, but we checked the airlines, and there's no sign of her having left."

WESTON WATCHED AS Daniela sagged in place. "Dear God," she said. "How can we possibly be surrounded by so many horrible people?"

"Not everybody is like your husband," he said, "and not everybody is like Angel."

"What about Grant, Gregory and Ginger?" she asked sarcastically.

"And what about all the other people around here, like the two mothers you spent time with today? Like the waitress at the restaurant? Like your sister? Like the detective who's helping us?"

She calmed down and mustered up a smile. "No, you're right. But it's all really sad, isn't it?" She got up, grabbed the dishes from the table and said, "I'll put on some coffee."

"Do you have tea?" he asked hopefully.

She stopped, turned to look at him and said, "Do you

like tea?"

"I love tea," he said. "I drink coffee all morning, but I do like tea in the evening."

She smiled. "I don't think I know another man who drinks tea."

"I spent some time in England and became quite a convert," he said.

She nodded. "Tea it is then." As she walked by, she bent down to kiss Sari on the cheek. "I don't know if you've noticed, but I think the dog is getting fed better than Sari is tonight." Laughing, she headed into the kitchen.

He wasn't sure if she would go cry while she did the dishes, but he figured she needed something to do with her hands. He shuffled closer to Sari, only to see Shambhala resting her chin on Sari's footrest Even as he watched, Sari reached down, picked up a piece of sausage and dropped it over the edge. Shambhala eagerly caught it midair.

He sighed. "Sari, doggy doesn't need more food."

She beamed at him. "Doggy, doggy." Then she picked up a whole handful of pasta and threw it on the floor.

He groaned, grabbed her bowl and, using her fork, tried to pop a few more bites into her mouth, but she wasn't having anything to do with it. He studied the bowl, then checked on the dog, her good eye giving him the most soulful look, staring back up at him.

"How am I supposed to know how much she ate if you'll clean up all the leftovers?" he asked the dog. But no answers were to be had from Shambhala.

When Daniela came back out, he said, "How do you know when Sari's eaten enough?"

She smiled and said, "If she hasn't, she'll want more later." She looked at the bowl and shrugged. "It's really hard to tell with Shambhala in the picture, isn't it?"

"That's what I was just trying to explain to them," he said, chuckling.

Daniela lifted the high chair tray up over Sari's head and scooped her up from the seat. "Regardless of who got what," she said, "it's obvious she's wearing a good portion of it as well."

But Sari was so happy and delighted to be feeding the doggy that, as soon as they moved away, she started screaming. Daniela wouldn't listen though and took her straight inside.

Weston looked down at Shambhala. "What will we do, girl?"

Shambhala just looked at him as if to say, *It's an easy solution, idiot.*

Weston wasn't sure he was ready for it, but then again he wasn't sure he had any choice either. Somehow this little girl and her mother had gotten inside his heart and had made a home for themselves right there. Not to mention Shambhala's entry into his life ...

He turned to Shambhala again. "Did you open the door for them?" he gently scolded. Shambhala's tail wagged like crazy with joy at his tone. He softly stroked her silky ears. "It's been a tough life, girl, but the rest of your years should be pretty easy."

"No, I don't think so," said a harsh voice from beside him. He turned to see Angel standing on the patio, holding a handgun against Daniela's head. Daniela, who held Sari in her arms, staring at him in terror.

"Well, hello, Angel," he said as he stood, pushing back his chair.

Shambhala looked from one to the other, not understanding. He stepped in front of the dog and gave her a hand signal to lie down. Then he put her on alert to watch.

He walked to Daniela and picked up Sari right out of her arms without Angel having a chance to say anything, then put her back in the high chair. As he walked past, he told Shambhala to guard. Shambhala sat up, her attention directly at Sari's side. He stepped over to Daniela, put an arm around her shoulder and tucked her up close, then took a step directly in front of the gun, so the barrel pressed against his chest. "Half the city is looking for you."

She stared at him, the gun now at an awkward angle because he'd stepped so close.

"What are you doing?" she cried out.

"What do you think I'm doing?" He reached up with a sudden move and snatched the gun from her hand. "Don't you *ever* bring a weapon near my family again," he snapped.

She shook her head and looked completely dumbfounded, her gaze going from Daniela to Weston and then over to Sari. "I don't know what little game you're playing at," she snarled, "but I don't have time for this shit."

"Why is that?" Weston said.

"Because I have to go, and I have to go now, and Sari is going with me."

"How will you make us do that?" he asked curiously. "I have your weapon, so you tell me how that'll work out for you."

She snorted. "Do you really think I came alone?" And just then two men burst through the kitchen, both with handguns.

He swore as he stared at them because this was a whole different story. Angel was one thing, but it was another to see these two strangers with cold dead looks in their eyes. "What do you want Sari for?" Daniela cried out. Her body was stiff, tense against him.

Angel laughed. "It doesn't matter," she said. "You don't get her any longer."

"You can't just kidnap another woman's child," Weston said. "What's the matter? Did your brother actually make it legit when he wasn't supposed to?"

"He was also supposed to get me a payout by sending her letters this last while. He got up on his high horse and refused to do it. He said he couldn't compromise his ethics, and the child was hers free and clear. But I wanted it set up so he was sending threatening letters so she would get used to it."

"Are you the one who sent the threatening letter to Grant and Ginger?"

"Well, that was Terry," she said, "but that's where I got the idea from, only my brother wouldn't do it."

"Of course not," Daniela said. "Sari is mine."

"But she's my daughter," Angel said, "and unless you've got fifty thousand dollars to give to me right now, she's leaving with me."

"Interesting figure," Weston said. "Who's buying her for that amount of money?"

"Doesn't matter who," she said, "but they have more money than Daniela, and Sari will have a better life."

"And you need the fifty thousand to pay off Terry, your loan shark? Is that it?"

She shot him a look full of hate. "That's exactly it. So you see? I don't have a choice here, even if I did want to keep her. She's the only asset I have."

"Except for one thing," Weston said. "She's not an asset. She's a child, and she's not yours anymore." He turned to look at the two men. "So, you from around here? Or did you come up to keep an eye on her?"

"They're Terry's men," she muttered, staring at them with almost hate in her gaze.

The two men motioned toward the baby. "Grab her and let's go," one said. "We've got a flight ready, and you know we've got to be on it. Otherwise there'll be hell to pay. Terry wants that money."

"And if he doesn't get it? Then what?" Weston asked.

"If he doesn't get it, she's dead," the guy said, shrugging. "You pay him back the money fair and square. Otherwise she pays the price."

"Wow," Weston said. "That's not much of a choice, is it?"

"Exactly," Angel said, "but it doesn't matter because I have to do this." She walked over to Sari, but Daniela raced ahead, only the men stepped forward, one grabbing Daniela and the other one walking toward Sari.

Weston knew Sari was covered because Shambhala was there to protect her. At least he hoped so. But with Angel and the two guys here, it might be more than Shambhala could do. One gunman was after Daniela and already had a chokehold around her neck and the gun against her temple. That was so they could use her to keep Weston compliant.

He casually spun around and, with a hand motion, told Shambhala to attack.

CHAPTER 18

I T WAS ALMOST like watching something in slow motion. Daniela was held with a gun to her head, panic in her throat, her heart slamming against her chest. She watched as Shambhala leaped from a seated position, her jaw wide open and—not reaching for his gun arm, like Daniela would have expected—went straight for the man's throat. He screamed and went down, fighting with the dog.

All of a sudden she heard nothing but an ugly gurgling. She shuddered and turned to look away. All this was happening as Angel now tried to get Sari out of her high chair. But Weston was right there too. Then suddenly he had Angel in a chokehold, glaring at the gunman beside her.

"I'll kill Angel," Weston snapped, "then you."

The gunman shrugged. "I don't give a shit. Those are my orders. If we don't get the money, we are supposed to take the baby and ditch Angel."

Angel stared at him, unable to speak, still choking under Weston's pressure around her neck. Weston eased his grip enough to let her stand to the side. There wasn't anything about this scenario he liked.

"What?" he said in response to her look. "Why do I need you? You don't even know the kid. The kid doesn't know you. I can listen to it scream just as good as you can." He sneered and without warning put a bullet in her head.

Weston was already on the move, looking for a distraction, and somehow he had the dog moving once more.

Daniela watched in horror as the dog raced toward them. The gunman turned his gun hand away from her and moved to point it at Shambhala, and she knew she had to stop that. She reached up with her leg, trying to kick his arm.

As he tightened the chokehold around her neck, everything in her world sank down to a black circle, but she was determined to stop him from shooting the dog who had already saved her daughter once. Then, all of a sudden, the arm was jerked away from her throat.

The dog had the gun arm this time, and there was Weston, landing one heavy punch in the gunman's face. After a second heavy punch, the guy went to his knees. With the third one, his nose shattered, and he went down screaming. Then he went quiet.

Weston stopped and talked to Shambhala. She looked at him, still growling with a bloodlust in her eyes that Daniela had never seen before. But, with simple hand gestures, Shambhala dropped the arm of the second man and came over to Weston, whining.

He cuddled her gently and whispered, "Good girl. That was a good girl. You did exactly what you were supposed to do."

Daniela ran to Sari, who was screaming at the top of her lungs in terror. Daniela picked up her daughter and wrapped her arms around her, holding her close. And then, not wanting to be away from Weston or Shambhala, she crouched beside the dog and the man. Weston wrapped up all three of them in his arms, and Shambhala licked Sari's face as she sobbed, each little hand clutching her furry friend. They all held each other like that for a long moment.

"Is it over?" Daniela whispered.

"Two dead probably, one not," he said. "I'm still hearing sounds from behind you."

She didn't want to look at the man whose throat had been ripped out because the blood was still pumping.

"There's nothing anybody can do for him," he said gently. "It'll be over fast. The other man, I think he's gone, but I don't know for sure though."

She shuddered and burrowed her face tight against him, while he tightened his arms and held them close. "I don't know how that happened," she whispered, "but, dear God, I just want it to be over."

"Except for this guy down beside us," he said, "it is. Angel is definitely dead."

"Is it wrong of me to be happy about that?" she whispered.

"No," he said, "that would be completely normal. But I need to phone the detective."

She nodded and pulled back so he could find his phone. But, with the armload he was cuddling, it was hard. He finally got his phone out, and she realized his hands were bloody, but he dialed the detective. She could hear the call as he explained what happened. The detective sounded shocked, if not horrified, and then resigned.

"I'm on the way," he said, "but, damn, I was really hoping to get home and have a meal with my family tonight."

"At least now we know where Angel is," Weston said. "You need to get an ambulance here for one guy. There's nothing to be done for the other one."

"I'll be there in ten," he said in a resigned voice.

Weston ended the call, while Daniela watched. She looked up at him and said, "Are we in trouble over this?"

He shook his head. "No, we were defending our family. That's all there is to it."

"What about Shambhala?" she asked, reaching out to stroke the beautiful dog who'd done so much to save her baby girl.

"Nope. She did what she was supposed to do too. If anybody would pay a price for that, it would be me because I gave her orders, but I don't think that will be a problem either."

She sighed gently. "You know what? The next time you suggest going on a date, I think we should do it," she said, "because, staying at home sucks."

He burst out laughing and said, "Listen. It'll be an ugly night here. Do you want to take Sari and go stay somewhere else, like with your sister or something?"

"I want to stay with you," she said.

"Good enough," he said. "I'll have to see if I can get you upstairs, while the men are working down here."

She nodded. "We will do what we need to do, but I wouldn't mind an early bedtime and at least some chance to de-stress."

It was crazy watching the organized chaos as the detective came in and took one look, then shook his head and got down to business. After she'd given her statement, she was allowed to go upstairs with Sari. Shambhala went along at her heels, not leaving Sari's side. And Daniela was beyond grateful. She owed the dog so much.

She was just thankful Sari was okay. The fact that Angel was gone was shocking but a blessing for their future.

Upstairs in her room, Daniela sat down and noticed the dress she'd planned to wear on their date. She shook her head. It wasn't that late, but it had been an exhausting day.

Needing something to keep her occupied, she gave Sari her bath and then tucked her into bed.

After just a few minutes of reading, Sari was fast asleep with Shambhala lying beside the bed.

Not wanting to leave her alone, Daniela sat here with her laptop, looking at various other US states. No way in hell she wanted to stay here now. She'd miss her sister, but it wasn't enough to keep her here. When her phone rang, and she saw her sister's number, she wondered if she wanted to answer it. Deciding to get it over with, she picked up the phone.

"What's going on?" Davida demanded.

"You wouldn't believe it if I could tell you," she said tiredly, "and I'm not sure what I'm even allowed to say." Still, she gave her the bare-bones story, cringing at her sister's cries with every new turn in the twisted tale.

"We're safe now. I'm upstairs, while the police are at work down below. Sari's in bed sleeping, and I'm sitting beside her with my laptop."

"Would you want to come here for the night?" her sister asked.

"No, but thank you," Daniela said. "I want to stay here with Weston. He's had a pretty rough time of it too."

"I was really wrong about him, wasn't I?"

"I don't know. He just defended the two of us against terrible odds, and we're not hurt," she said in disbelief. "But two dead people are downstairs, and another is severely injured."

"I hope that one dies too," Davida said. "What has happened to this town?"

"I don't know," she said, "but I'm more than ready to move."

At that, her sister gasped. "Seriously?"

"Yes," she said, emotionally exhausted. "I don't know where yet. But I don't want to spend another winter up here." There was an odd silence, and then Daniela swore she could hear her sister's frown.

"Why?"

"It just seems like a fresh start would be good. I'll miss you though."

"Brian's being transferred," her sister said in a rush.

Daniela froze. "Seriously?"

"Yes," she said. "To New Mexico."

"Oh, my God. You're moving anyway."

"I'm sorry I didn't tell you sooner. I didn't know how." She sounded defensive.

"Well, now you have," she said. "And I made the decision to move regardless."

"You could come to New Mexico," Davida said hopefully.

"Maybe, I don't know."

"Where is Weston from?"

"Most recently, Santa Fe," she said, laughing.

Her sister gasped. Then started to laugh too. "Okay, so maybe I was really wrong. It sounds like a fated meeting to me."

"Not to mention we had the DNA testing rushed, and he is definitely Sari's father."

"Oh my," she said. "And Angel is gone forever, right?"

"Yes," she said. "And good riddance. She was planning to sell Sari for fifty thousand dollars to pay off a loan shark."

"Oh, my God," Davida cried out. "How low can anybody go?"

"Apparently very low," Daniela said, suddenly super-tired. "Listen. I'll hang up now. I think I hear Weston coming up the stairs."

"Well, my offer still stands, if you want a place for the night. I can't believe the police will let you stay there."

"I don't know that they will, but I'd like to stay if I can." With that, she hung up. She walked to the doorway to see Weston looking into the master bedroom, and, not seeing her, turning toward Sari's room. She smiled up at him. "Are you okay?

"I am," he said, "but it'll be chaos downstairs for quite a few hours. We can go to a hotel, you know?"

She frowned, thinking about it and then said, "What would you like to do?"

"It would have to be a hotel that takes dogs," he said. "Otherwise I'd rather stay here."

"Agreed," she said. "I'd like to get a steak just for Shambhala."

He smiled and joined Daniela in Sari's room, then reached out a hand to the dog, who even now was at his daughter's bedside. "She has certainly earned her keep," he admitted.

"Angel didn't admit to killing her brother though, did she?"

"Not in so many words," he said. "I have no doubt that's what happened. But I don't know if there's a way to prove it."

"I wonder if we'll ever find out."

"I don't know. I think the detective wants me to leave town and fast," he said with a smile. "And you? What does your rental agreement say?"

"It's pretty standard," she said. "I have to give a month's notice."

He nodded. "And the end of the month is coming up."

"Yes," she said. "So I have to pay for next month, but I could leave any time after that."

"And will you?" he asked, leaning against the doorjamb with his hands in his pockets.

"Maybe," she said. "If I had a reason to and a place to go. I just found out from my sister"—motioning at her cell phone—"that her husband is being transferred, moving to New Mexico."

"Wow," he said. "It's hard to argue with that."

"Maybe," she said. "I don't know what it's like there."

"Well, it's not nearly as cold," he said with half a smile.

She grinned and nodded. "Good point," she said.

He looked around at the furnishings. "How much of this do you want to keep?"

She found herself considering the logistics of moving an entire household that far. "I'm not sure I care about very much of it. And how hard would it be to drive it all that far? Or should I just let it all go and fly?"

"That stuff we can worry about later," he said. "You should sleep now, if you can. I don't know that you want to sleep in your bedroom now though, if she's already asleep here."

"No," she said, "I can't sleep yet, but I thought I'd stay here." She nodded to the rocker, near Sari's crib, pointing out the daybed too.

"Good enough. I'll go back downstairs and keep an eye on things. We'll have to tell the landlord too."

She wrinkled her nose up at that. "That won't be fun."

He smiled. "I think it's the law on something like this, but I don't know. There's some damage to the patio for sure. I don't know if we can get the bloodstains out."

"It's still better this happened outside than inside," she muttered.

"Do you want me to bring you a cup of tea?"

"Yes," she said. "I would love that." And she watched as he disappeared. Something was just so damn special about a man who looked after you like that.

It was a while before he returned, almost an hour, but he was carrying a cup of tea. "Sorry it's so late," he said.

"That's fine. How is it going?"

"Well, the bodies are gone. The forensics guys are working still."

"What about the guy you punched out?"

"That's both good news and bad news," he said, squatting in front of her to study his daughter, who still slept soundly in her crib. Shambhala reached over and nudged him with her muzzle. Instantly he stroked and caressed her long silky fur. "He didn't make it."

She gasped.

"I guess, when I hit him, and his nose exploded, a piece of the bone went into his brain."

She took several long, slow breaths as her mind processed the information. "Once again," she said, "I feel like it's wrong to be happy about it, but it seems like the best thing for everybody."

"I don't have a problem with it. That man came here, held a gun on my family and was trying to kidnap my daughter. As far as I'm concerned, having them all dead is the best way." A shout came from downstairs, and Weston said, "I've got to go see what they want."

She smiled. "We'll be fine here. Thanks for the tea."

He nodded and disappeared downstairs.

ANOTHER TWO HOURS later he made it back upstairs again, and, when he walked into Sari's room, Daniela was stretched out on the floor with her feet propped up on the edge of the crib, sound asleep too. He winced because he knew she would be damn sore in the morning, sleeping like that. He walked into the master bedroom and pulled back the covers, thinking he could wake her up and bring her to bed, but she resisted all forms of easy wakening. He smiled because she slept just as heavily as Sari did. Finally he scooped her up, carried her to the master bedroom and laid her down on the bed.

Quickly he stripped her of her outside layer of clothing, leaving on her bra and panties, and tucking her under the covers. Instead of doing what he wanted to do, which was crawling in beside her, he reached down and gave her a quick kiss on the cheek. He left a lamp on low.

Then he went into Sari's room and looked over at the small crib, where his daughter still slept. Would she panic if she woke up and didn't see her mom? Would Daniela panic if she woke up and didn't see her baby? The crib was on wheels, so that was an easy solution. Moving quietly through the hallway, he wheeled Sari's bed so it was beside Daniela. Shambhala totally agreed with the concept and, when Weston picked up the rug she'd been sleeping on and put it between the two women, Shambhala took up a position between them. Weston bent down and gave her a cuddle.

He headed back downstairs once more, and, when the authorities finally left, he locked up and returned upstairs, heading toward his own bed in the guest room. And then found Daniela sitting up, rubbing the sleep from her eyes.

He walked in and said, "Hey, sorry, I didn't mean to wake you."

"It's okay," she whispered. "What's going on downstairs?"

"They're gone. It's quite a mess, and we'll have lots of cleaning to do tomorrow, but it's over."

She smiled and looked down. "Did you put me to bed?"

"Yes," he said, "you looked so uncomfortable the way you were lying." Then she smiled at Sari's crib beside her. She looked up at him and said, "You are the sweetest man."

He shook his head. "I don't know about that, but you need to get more rest."

She patted the bed beside her. "Curl up," she said. "We all need rest, and nobody needs to be alone."

"That would be dangerous," he said with a half smile. "I was on my best behavior putting you to bed, but I won't be on good behavior if I get in too."

She gave him a slow dawning smile. "I've been on good behavior for one hell of a long time. I really don't mind letting loose a little tonight."

"Are you sure?" he asked, studying her carefully.

"It's got nothing to do with tonight and nothing to do with Sari," she said. "It has everything to do with you. I don't think I've ever met a man quite like you."

He frowned, still unsure.

She looked up at him, slowly pushed the covers back and slipped out of bed. Still wearing only her panties and bra, she walked toward him, her hands sliding up his chest. "You know you're wearing too many clothes, right?"

His grin flashed. "I can take care of that in no time," he said, "but I don't want this to be a reaction, you know, to—"

CHAPTER 19

"T O ALL THAT violence?" Daniela said. "I get it. Partly it is a reaction because, if there's anything that one needs to affirm in the face of so much death, it is life. And, if there's anybody I'd like to do that with, it would be you." She tugged him into Sari's room, her fingers already busy undoing the buttons on his shirt, then tugging the material out of his jeans. When she got his shirt off his chest, she stopped and stared because he was heavily muscled every-where. Even the multiple crisscrossing of scars didn't diminish the sense of power exuding from him. She stared in astonishment, her hands stroking the huge muscles across his pecks.

As she stroked her finger down to his belt buckle, his belly automatically retracted, and a massive six-pack showed up. "Wow," she said. "I've never been a girl who cared about jocks, but, man, oh, man, there's something about all these muscles." She gently stroked her hands over the ridges and hills until he grabbed her hands and tugged her close. She could see the worry still in his eyes.

"Are you sure?" he said, his breath catching in the back of his throat.

She smiled. "Never more sure in my life," she whispered, stretching up on her tiptoes, but still she could only reach his chin. She kissed him gently.

He leaned down to give her a kiss on the lips. The first kiss was tentative and gentle, more of a searching kiss to see if there was a response. And what a response there was, as she could feel her heart slamming against her ribs and then her body straining to get closer to his. She threw her arms around his neck and passionately kissed him back.

His arms wrapped around her and held her tight.

With her pressed against his bare chest, she could already feel his response. She loved it. She loved everything about it. She'd missed being held, missed making love and missed being close to somebody. She hadn't been with anyone since her husband, thinking she could never trust another man. But instinctively she knew this would be a man she could trust, not just for now but forever.

When he finally stepped back, he slipped off the rest of his clothes, and she unclipped her bra so she stood there just in tiny panties. But, even then, she stopped, amazed when she saw all of him. His quads were massive and, of course, the rest of him made her smile. She reached out, her fingers wrapping around his erection. He sucked in his breath, his hands going to hers to hold her there and to stop the movement.

"If you do that," he said, "it'll be over far too soon."

"Well, I highly doubt it'll be the end anyway. I suspect you're good for more than one round," she teased.

He gave her a wicked smile. "Why don't we find out?"

Before she realized what he intended, he picked her up and tossed her on the daybed, where she let out a startled squeak. She clapped her hand over her mouth as she realized her daughter slept just one door away. She'd never made love to a man with her daughter in the house before outside of Charlie.

He grinned. "Now you don't have to be as quiet," he said.

With two quick snaps, her tiny panties were gone. He stopped, his eyes going hot as he studied every inch of her nude body. "You are so tiny," he marveled, his hands spreading across her sunken belly.

"I'm hardly tiny."

"You are," he said. "Long, lean and beautiful."

She could hear the fervor in his voice and the passion coating his tones, and she loved it. She stretched out in front of him, her arms over her head. "I don't know how much peace and quiet we'll have—"

"So *get on with it*, is that it?" he teased in a whisper as he came down on the bed beside her. He knelt between her legs, staring at her. "You're so beautiful."

She laughed, completely natural and comfortable in this state. "It seems almost disrespectful to make love," she said, "with all the horrible events earlier."

"No," he said. "It has nothing to do with it. That was death. This is rebirth." He bent down, wrapped his arms under her and gently kissed her. Then he worked his way down her neck, her collarbone, her arm and right to her fingertips, kissing and caressing every inch of her.

She twisted and sighed, moaning with joy and passion, and, when he finally worked his way back up the other side of her, she was already mindless jelly. "I don't care how long you do this, and we can go all night, but I really, really, *really* want you inside me right now."

Before she had a chance to say anything else, he was seated right at the heart of her. Her body arched naturally, her muscles tense and struggling to relax and to accept this new force within her. He stilled and waited, his hands gently massaging her hips and her thighs. He murmured against her neck, "Are you okay?"

She took a deep breath, shifted her position and then nodded. "It's been a long time."

He leaned over her, smiled and whispered, "Good, but it won't be very long after this." And he kissed her, his tongue sliding deep within and mimicking the same motion as his hips as he started to move. She shuddered beneath him, her temperature already escalating back to where it had been before his entry. She kissed him tenderly at first, but soon there was no tenderness, just heat. It was passion; it was tumultuous emotions and pulsating nerves.

When he finally held her at the precipice, she whispered, "Now, please, dear God, now!"

He slid his fingers down between them to find the little nub and sent her flying off the cliff. As she floated free of her body, consumed by that kaleidoscope of emotions and nerve endings, she heard him groan above her, before collapsing beside her. He held her close and wrapped up in his arms as she lay against him.

"This was not quite what I expected when I came to Alaska," he whispered. "I had wished …"

She chuckled. "Then it's a good thing you came up here. I always knew it was important that you did. I just didn't know why."

"Well, it's important," he said, "and what's most important is what we do with it now."

She looked up at him. "Everything that's happened since you arrived here has been so crazy. It doesn't seem real."

He leaned over and kissed her hard. "Does that seem real?"

"Yes," she said, gently rubbing her nose against his.

"This is very real."

"And Sari's real," he said, "and Shambhala. So it looks to me like we have a family."

She stopped, her eyebrows shooting up.

"Well, you're Sari's mom," he said, "and I'm Sari's dad. And obviously Shambhala is Sari's guardian angel."

Her smile was breathtaking when she heard that. "Oh, I like that," she said. "What does it all mean though?" She pushed, looking for more from him.

"I don't know," he said, "but to me it sounds like a new beginning."

She stopped and looked up at him, and tears came to her eyes. "You know I'm all for a new beginning," she whispered. "It seems like I've had nothing but endings since I've been in Alaska."

"Not true," he said, "and, even if it were, it doesn't matter because I highly suggest that we leave all the bad stuff behind, and the four of us go start all over again somewhere new. I'd like to go back to New Mexico, but, if you want to go somewhere else, I'm totally okay with that too."

"All right." She looked up at him. "Is it really that easy?"

"No," he said. "The thing about easy is it's not always worth doing. It's the things that you really want, that you really have to work for, that are worth doing. And this"—he gestured down the hall to his daughter and back down at Daniela—"is something I really want. So you can count on the fact I'll really work hard to make it happen."

She slid her arms around his neck and chest. "You're saying all the right words. It's just happening so fast."

He nodded, nuzzling her cheek. "Exactly. It's happened fast, and, therefore, it's right. I don't do this with everybody," he said. "I know you're probably thinking of Angel and a one-night stand many moons ago. I was a different man back then. I was on leave. I was drunk. I took what was offered. That was a whole different story than right now."

She searched his gaze as he leaned over, kissing her again.

"Why do you think it took me so long to come to Alaska and see you?"

She frowned. "I figured you didn't want to have anything to do with us."

"No. It's because I knew how important it could be, and I wanted to make sure I was ready and prepared for the changes this would bring in my life."

"But you didn't know this would happen," she protested.

He gave her that slow dawning smile, and she stared at him in wonder. "I didn't know for sure, but I wondered, and I'm very happy to say that this is exactly what I had wished for."

Her eyes filled with tears as she threw her arms around his neck again and whispered, "It's what I wished for too."

"In that case, why don't we find out if wishes can come true?"

EPILOGUE

I T WAS A new stage of life for him—this sitting around, doing what he wanted, helping out others basically by choice instead of having a regimented lifestyle. When Greyson Morgenstein had been in the military, a Navy SEAL no less, he had been on training missions, more training, more fitness, more missions. And after his accident that ruined his back, damaged his shoulder and took off part of his foot, it had seemed like it was so much the same, and yet so different, because it was therapy, then doctors, more tests, more physical fitness, more of everything, but everything on a schedule.

Since he'd been released, his back was as good as it would get, just needed more strengthening. His shoulder was functional, not pretty, but who said that was even part of his life anymore? He learned to walk with just half the foot, and who knew that would be such a pain? But he was better off than so many of the other guys.

He lifted his coffee mug and stretched. He was out along the back of Geir's house. They'd been working on building decks on a bunch of the guy's places. And Greyson really enjoyed the camaraderie of being here, the sense of belonging, and yet without the pressure to do anything.

He was living off his benefits at the moment, while he tried to assess what the hell he wanted to do with his life.

The only thing he really couldn't do would be heavy construction, but not much else held him back.

He'd been a trainer within the military, so management might be something he could do. But he didn't think he wanted anything to do with that kind of pressure, any more of that stress. He loved animals, had worked briefly with the K9 department in the military, but had wanted a much more personal relationship with the animals than the handlers were allowed to have. He'd seen various animal rescues that interested him, but that wasn't a way to make money.

When Geir sat down beside him, Greyson said, "It's a nice deal you've got going here."

Geir nodded slowly. "It is. It was a long time coming. What we've got, we've built ourselves."

Greyson didn't say anything else, just sipped his coffee.

"What do you want for your future?" Geir asked.

Greyson shrugged. "Something different, something more peaceful than the navy and all the missions. Something still helping out, I guess, but without the stress, without the schedule, without the chaos."

Geir nodded. "You know not too many people would understand that."

"Well, I sure as hell hope some could." He shook his head. "I want to stop and smell the roses a little more."

Geir grinned. "You need a wife for that."

"Is that what helped you?"

Geir thought about it, then nodded. "A lot of my adjustments came from her being in my life—having that other perspective—plus having the guys at my side as we decided what we wanted to do, moving forward. All of us having physical disabilities made the world look at us differently." He shook his head. "It makes you reassess."

"It does, indeed," Greyson said.

"How do you feel about animals?"

"Love them. I was just thinking it's too bad I can't set up a rescue, but they don't make any money so …"

"What kind of rescue?"

"I don't know. I'm particular to dogs, but I'm a cat guy too," he said with a quirk of his lips.

"Interesting."

"That sounded like you have something going on in the back of your head."

"We've been working some K9 files. We've had a really good success rate, but this next one? We just don't have a lot of information on it."

"What are the K9 files?"

And he listened while Geir explained about the War Dog Division shutting down this part of the department, and a bunch of these dogs having been lost in the system.

"Those dogs give their lives in many instances," Greyson said. "They certainly give the best years of their physical lives, and they deserve to have a decent ending to it."

"Which is why we agreed to help on a *pro bono* basis," Geir said. "What we now have is Kona. A Belgian Malinois female, who was shipped to Denver but somehow ended up in Hawaii."

"That doesn't even compute," Greyson said, staring at him in surprise.

"Right?"

"So has she been shipped back to Denver?"

"No, she was picked up, supposed to go to a foster setup for a few nights, until someone could arrange her trip home, only she disappeared overnight."

"Well, that could be a good thing," Greyson said. "A lot

of people don't agree with shelters."

"This was a rescue. She had her own run. She should have been just fine there," Geir said. "What we can't do is ignore this. We need to know that whoever stole the dog is looking after her and that the dog will have the best life possible."

"What about legalities in this one?"

"An adoptive family was lined up in Denver. We didn't have anybody in Hawaii."

"So, if I do find the dog, and I do find that it's in a good home, am I supposed to rip it away and send it to Denver?"

Geir thought about that for a long moment as he studied his coffee cup. "No," he finally said. "I think the baseline here is that we go with whatever is in the best interests of the dog."

"So, go find the dog, track down whoever stole it, figure out why and what they're doing with it and if the dog will be okay?" He looked around at the yard he spent the last few days working at and said, "Hawaii could be good."

Geir looked at him and smiled. "Any connection for you?"

"Grandparents. They used to live in New York, and then, one day, it's like they snapped, sold everything and moved to Hawaii."

"Hey, I'm not sure that's such a bad idea," Geir said, "but honestly, if you'll be in one of the big cities, I'm not sure there's any difference."

"They're on one of the outer islands, I believe," he said. "It might be time to find out."

"Exactly."

"What airport did the dog disappear from?"

"It was flown into Lanai Airport, and then it was at the

Freedom shelter. That's the last known location we have."

He nodded. "How long ago?"

"Now that we are actually delving into this case, it's possible the trail ran cold a long time ago. The dog has been missing for just over three months."

"So long enough to bond but not enough to bond well."

"Depends on the circumstances, as you know," Geir said.

Greyson nodded. "Some situations require immediate bonding. But those are usually the ugly situations. Danger, strife, violence, something along that line."

"Exactly. So maybe we need to find out just what's going on in that poor dog's life."

Greyson chuckled. "I think I can handle this one."

Geir looked at him, grinned and said, "*Think* so?"

"I know so. Mission accepted."

This concludes Book 8 of The K9 Files: Weston.

Read about Greyson: The K9 Files, Book 9

THE K9 FILES: GREYSON (BOOK #9)

Welcome to the all new K9 Files series reconnecting readers with the unforgettable men from SEALs of Steel in a new series of action packed, page turning romantic suspense that fans have come to expect from USA TODAY Bestselling author Dale Mayer. Pssst… you'll meet other favorite characters from SEALs of Honor and Heroes for Hire too!

Combining a trip to see his grandparents with hunting down a K9 dog sounds like a good excuse at the time to Greyson. Somehow the K9 had been accidentally flow halfway around the world in the wrong direction and then lost. Finding the dog wasn't easy, but Greyson follows the trail of destruction the same as the K9 does … and finds the female shepherd protecting a mother and child … So not what he expected.

Jessica didn't understand why the dog was always around, but the dog was plain scary. Although not as much as everything else going on in her life right now. Most things she blames on her ex-husband, but was he this mean? With her toddler son to protect, she knows she can't make a mistake that will bring them harm.

As the events escalate, it doesn't take long to decide who was on her side and who … wasn't.

Find Book 9 here!
To find out more visit Dale Mayer's website.
http://smarturl.it/DMSGreyson

Author's Note

Thank you for reading Weston: The K9 Files, Book 8! If you enjoyed the book, please take a moment and leave a short review.

Dear reader,

I love to hear from readers, and you can contact me at my website: www.dalemayer.com or at my Facebook author page. To be informed of new releases and special offers, sign up for my newsletter or follow me on BookBub. And if you are interested in joining Dale Mayer's Reader Group, here is the Facebook sign up page.
https://smarturl.it/DaleMayerFBGroup

Cheers,
Dale Mayer

Get THREE Free Books Now!

Have you met the SEALS of Honor?

SEALs of Honor Books 1, 2, and 3. Follow the stories of brave, badass warriors who serve their country with honor and love their women to the limits of life and death.

Read Mason, Hawk, and Dane right now for FREE.

Go here and tell me where to send them!
http://smarturl.it/EthanBofB

About the Author

Dale Mayer is a USA Today bestselling author best known for her Psychic Visions and Family Blood Ties series. Her contemporary romances are raw and full of passion and emotion (Second Chances, SKIN), her thrillers will keep you guessing (By Death series), and her romantic comedies will keep you giggling (It's a Dog's Life and Charmin Marvin Romantic Comedy series).

She honors the stories that come to her – and some of them are crazy and break all the rules and cross multiple genres!

To go with her fiction, she also writes nonfiction in many different fields with books available on resume writing, companion gardening and the US mortgage system. She has recently published her Career Essentials Series. All her books are available in print and ebook format.

Connect with Dale Mayer Online

Dale's Website – www.dalemayer.com
Facebook Personal – https://smarturl.it/DaleMayerFacebook
Instagram – https://smarturl.it/DaleMayerInstagram
BookBub – https://smarturl.it/DaleMayerBookbub
Facebook Fan Page – https://smarturl.it/DaleMayerFBFanPage
Goodreads – https://smarturl.it/DaleMayerGoodreads

Also by Dale Mayer

Published Adult Books:

Hathaway House

Aaron, Book 1

Brock, Book 2

Cole, Book 3

Denton, Book 4

Elliot, Book 5

Finn, Book 6

Gregory, Book 7

Heath, Book 8

Iain, Book 9

Jaden, Book 10

Keith, Book 11

The K9 Files

Ethan, Book 1

Pierce, Book 2

Zane, Book 3

Blaze, Book 4

Lucas, Book 5

Parker, Book 6

Carter, Book 7

Weston, Book 8

Greyson, Book 9

Lovely Lethal Gardens

Arsenic in the Azaleas, Book 1
Bones in the Begonias, Book 2
Corpse in the Carnations, Book 3
Daggers in the Dahlias, Book 4
Evidence in the Echinacea, Book 5
Footprints in the Ferns, Book 6
Gun in the Gardenias, Book 7
Handcuffs in the Heather, Book 8
Ice Pick in the Ivy, Book 9
Jewels in the Juniper, Book 10

Psychic Vision Series

Tuesday's Child
Hide 'n Go Seek
Maddy's Floor
Garden of Sorrow
Knock Knock…
Rare Find
Eyes to the Soul
Now You See Her
Shattered
Into the Abyss
Seeds of Malice
Eye of the Falcon
Itsy-Bitsy Spider
Unmasked
Deep Beneath
From the Ashes
Stroke of Death
Psychic Visions Books 1–3
Psychic Visions Books 4–6

Heroes for Hire

SEALs of Steel

Laszlo: SEALs of Steel, Book 5
Geir: SEALs of Steel, Book 6
Jager: SEALs of Steel, Book 7
The Final Reveal: SEALs of Steel, Book 8
SEALs of Steel, Books 1–4
SEALs of Steel, Books 5–8
SEALs of Steel, Books 1–8

The Mavericks
Kerrick, Book 1
Griffin, Book 2
Jax, Book 3
Beau, Book 4
Asher, Book 5
Ryker, Book 6
Miles, Book 7
Nico, Book 8
Keane, Book 9
Lennox, Book 10
Gavin, Book 11
Shane, Book 12

Bullard's Battle Series
Ryland's Reach, Book 1
Cain's Cross, Book 2
Eton's Escape, Book 3
Garret's Gambit, Book 4
Kano's Keep, Book 5
Fallon's Flaw, Book 6
Quinn's Quest, Book 7
Bullard's Beauty, Book 8

Collections
Dare to Be You…
Dare to Love…
Dare to be Strong…
RomanceX3

Standalone Novellas
It's a Dog's Life
Riana's Revenge
Second Chances

Published Young Adult Books:

Family Blood Ties Series
Vampire in Denial
Vampire in Distress
Vampire in Design
Vampire in Deceit
Vampire in Defiance
Vampire in Conflict
Vampire in Chaos
Vampire in Crisis
Vampire in Control
Vampire in Charge
Family Blood Ties Set 1–3
Family Blood Ties Set 1–5
Family Blood Ties Set 4–6
Family Blood Ties Set 7–9
Sian's Solution, A Family Blood Ties Series Prequel
    Novelette

Design series
Dangerous Designs
Deadly Designs
Darkest Designs
Design Series Trilogy

Standalone
In Cassie's Corner
Gem Stone (a Gemma Stone Mystery)
Time Thieves

Published Non-Fiction Books:

Career Essentials
Career Essentials: The Résumé
Career Essentials: The Cover Letter
Career Essentials: The Interview
Career Essentials: 3 in 1

CPSIA information can be obtained
at www.ICGtesting.com
Printed in the USA
LVHW010428300620
659309LV00012B/1526